Heaven May Have Quills

Jack D. Osenbaugh

Pentland Press, Inc.
England • USA • Scotland

PUBLISHED BY PENTLAND PRESS, INC.
5124 Bur Oak Circle, Raleigh, North Carolina 27612
United States of America
919-782-0281

ISBN 1-57197-085-1
Library of Congress Catalog Card Number 97-069234

Printed in the United States of America

I dedicate this book to my wife Betty and to my three sons, Chris, Cory, and Casey. They were a very important part of my life and enjoyment when we lived in Wyoming. I hope to return someday.

Chapter One

Tyler was a tall, well-built, slender man who would see his thirty-seventh birthday the middle of the next month. Having been divorced for a little over seven years, much of his leisure time was spent keeping his body, now a few pounds over what he perceived to be his ideal weight, as physically fit as possible. His broad shoulders, long blond hair, and fading tan presented a respectable view. Except for the large half-moon-shaped scar on his right shoulder, Tyler was an attractive gentleman.

The scar was the only trophy Tyler had from his brief career in the NFL, which had ended abruptly during his rookie year as a highly touted linebacker from Penn State. Tyler often thought about the horrible career-ending event, bringing flashes of pain to his mind. He had been a determined rookie, putting out one hundred percent to secure a treasured spot on the defensive unit for Cleveland. Thank God he had gotten his business degree. The healing process was slow, causing the coaches to move him to number four on the depth chart. Ultimately, he had been released before the end of his first season.

Feeling down and defeated, Tyler had spent the rest of the fall and most of the winter hanging out in his small hometown of Lynch, Ohio, where he met his wife-to-be, Susan Kindle. Susan had attended Lynch High School with Tyler; she was a ninth-grade student when Tyler graduated and left the little town to attend Penn State University on an athletic scholarship.

Susan was the only child of a Presbyterian minister, and her life was very structured and strict during her adolescent years. Her loving father died suddenly from congestive heart failure during her first year in college. A bright and aggressive student, Susan had received several scholarships, but was forced to attend a small college in Tennessee, where she could live with her aunt. She managed to get through her freshman year, and reluctantly enrolled for her sophomore year. Before the fall quarter commenced, however, she was called home to assist her mother, who had been diagnosed with leukemia. Her mother survived the winter and died in the early spring, leaving Susan without enough funds to go back to school.

Susan managed to secure a job in the local library and continued to live in her mother's home, which fortunately had been paid off with the mortgage insurance that her father had purchased. Her job barely paid enough to cover the utilities and buy food, and Susan's life was quite boring and uneventful. There was no time, and certainly no money, for socializing and meeting new friends.

Tyler was a godsend for Susan. He was handsome, and also experienced, as most college-educated men are. He provided a feeling of security for Susan, as well as a few laughs. Their relationship was exciting and developed quickly. After three short months of romance, Susan was shocked to find herself madly in love with Tyler.

They were married, and Tyler moved into Susan's home in the fall. Tyler worked for a local brokerage firm and earned a respectable salary. He was a personable young man, and securing clients was easy for him. Though the small town lacked many clients who could afford to invest more than a few hundred dollars, Tyler nonetheless did very well.

Susan and Tyler were extremely happy during the early years of their marriage. Their life together seemed grand. Tyler was promoted to senior account executive and was earning a very respectable salary. He joined the local country club, and with his natural athletic ability he soon became a great golfer, playing every Wednesday afternoon and at least one day each weekend. Tyler quickly worked his way into the circle of the club's better golfers and more elite professionals. Meanwhile, Susan was promoted to head librarian at the public library, and socialized with the wives of the men at the country club.

Susan and Tyler's life became quite trendy and social. The thought of having children constantly crossed Susan's mind, but she was utterly disappointed when she mentioned it to Tyler. He was an extremely aggressive, goal-oriented individual who wanted nothing more than to prove he could be the very best investment account executive in the business. To his mind, there was no time for being a parent. Miss a meeting? Lose a client? Not a chance. This was his life, and there was no way Tyler would jeopardize his future by taking time from work to raise a family.

Life sped on at the country club, with social parties and weekend trips to expensive resorts. Susan and Tyler's love for each other faded and gradually died. Life became a dreadful struggle for Susan. She was raised as the child of a very conservative minister, and she was quite uncomfortable with her new lifestyle. The continual parties, drinking, and expensive social events were not for her. She merely wanted to settle down, raise a family, and be a housewife to a husband who could enjoy a routine, boring lifestyle.

Susan and Tyler grew further and further apart, until at last they were forced to recognize their incompatibility. They decided it was time to divorce.

Afterward, Tyler, who felt guilty and not at all compassionate, found that visiting the country club and seeing all his married friends was lackluster. He couldn't handle seeing Susan around town, and was jealous and hurt when she started seeing the Lynch High School vice principal. Susan and her new companion seemed very happy together. Tyler was devastated when he saw the vice principal's vehicle at Susan's home one morning on his way to work. It was painfully apparent that he had spent the night with her.

Tyler couldn't stay. He decided he must leave Lynch. He loved the outdoors, and he wanted badly to be a part of it. However, his inner drive to succeed kept him from becoming a full-blown mountaineer. He was torn between his love for the outdoors and his drive to be a successful businessman. He realized he must have funds to survive, and so for the time being getting a job seemed to be the only choice for Tyler.

After several phone calls and a trip to Chicago for an interview, Tyler secured a staff position with the brokerage firm of Jenson and Jenson, one of the more reputable investment banking firms in the city. He was extremely fortunate to have contacted the firm at about the time that Alex Raddison unexpectedly announced his early retirement. Mr. Raddison would be leaving behind entire files of investment portfolios that he had spent the past twelve years developing. With a few new clients, Tyler would be able to enjoy an income that would provide quite an affluent lifestyle. Without delay, he moved to Chicago to join the firm.

Chapter Two

Garris Jenson, the older brother in the firm of Jenson and Jenson, was a distinguished gentleman who appeared to be in his early to mid-sixties. His gray hair was cropped and curly in the back and meticulously brushed on the sides. He wore fashionable wire-rim spectacles, perched about halfway down his long, pointed nose. Garris was attired in a tailored, gray pinstriped, double-breasted suit accented with a tasteful blue tie with red polka dots. His breast pocket was stuffed with a matching puffy handkerchief of the same expensive silk. His black wingtip shoes bore a lustrous shine less than a few hours old, and the Rolex watch on his wrist, worn loose, flopped around as he extended his hand to make his greeting. Mr. Jenson projected an image of cash—real money, the green stuff.

"Welcome to Jenson and Jenson. It is a pleasure to have you join our staff." Tyler reached for Mr. Jenson's hand and gave it a firm, confident shake. Jenson continued: "I read your resume, and I think I remember you, Tyler—Penn State, wasn't it? I follow college football very closely—have for thirty years. What happened to you after college? I heard you were drafted in the first few rounds, then I never heard of you again. Couldn't you stand the heat, or weren't you good enough?"

What a terribly crass thing to say, Tyler thought. Screw this old man; who the hell does he think he is anyway?

Jenson went on: "The NFL doesn't tolerate half-assed, mediocre talent."

Tyler was ready to go off on the old geezer, but instead he kept his cool and walked over to the overstuffed, plush velvet visitor's chair and turned around to face Mr. Jenson. "Got hurt—dislocated and fractured my shoulder. Never made it to the first game. I think I would have had a shot, if I had not gotten hurt. By the time it healed, I was history. So I forgot about football and took up golf. It's not nearly as painful, and you don't have to play in front of eighty thousand screaming, biased fans who are waiting for you to step on your dick so they can boo you off the field."

Jenson looked down his nose through his spectacles and asked, "You a good golfer? What's your handicap—legitimate?"

Tyler grinned and responded, "Used to be a seven, but I haven't played much the last six months, so I would guess I could play to about a ten or so right now."

Tyler was setting himself up in case Jenson was going to challenge him to a game. Surprisingly, Mr. Jenson responded, "Well, I don't have any use for that damnable, time-killing habit. Too damn busy trying to figure out how to keep the rest of my staff off the golf course and kicking ass in the investment market. Can you work sixty hours a week and forget about golf?"

Tyler brushed his fingers through his long blond hair and looked Mr. Jenson directly in the eye. "Whatever your heart desires. All I ask is to be properly compensated for my contribution to your continued success."

The other Jenson, Garris' brother, entered the room from the hall door leading to the plush offices which housed the account management staff, made up of about twenty people. This Jenson was rather casually dressed in a pair of double-pleated, cuffed slacks topped with a beige pigskin suede sports coat and a gray-blue ascot. The smart outfit was balanced by beige brushed pigskin loafers.

"Hank Jenson. And you must be Tyler, the new account executive, from some place in—Indiana, is it?"

"Ohio," Tyler said. "Lynch, Ohio."

"Pleased to meet you, and welcome to our staff." Hank looked Tyler up and down before asking, "Just get to town?"

"I arrived on Saturday and spent the entire weekend moving into my townhouse over on Front Street, Chadwick Place. Ever heard of it?"

Hank turned his head to gaze out the window. "Yes, I think I have. A tall, brown building with a wrought-iron double gate in front. I've never been in the place, but I hear it's not too bad. Just make sure you have good security. This damn town is dreadfully infested with crime, all kinds. You can't even walk down the street after dark without some bastard trying to either lift your wallet, stick a knife in you, or both. Too damn much worry for an old man like me. I go straight home and lock my door. I don't come out until it's time to go to work, unless I take some protection with me—you know, some big strong bodyguard or something."

After a fashionable lunch in a small French restaurant, Tyler was introduced to the women in the secretarial pool and the large staff of account managers. Next, he was shown to his office, which was lavishly furnished with a solid oak desk and an overstuffed brown leather chair. The walls were tastefully decorated with landscape scenes of what appeared to be the Swiss Alps. The credenza behind the desk was loaded with an IBM personal computer, a twelve-button telephone, and a Hewlett Packard plain-paper fax machine.

Tyler turned to Garris Jenson and asked, "Are all the accounts that Mr. Raddison managed in the files? Will Mr. Raddison be available to introduce me, or am I to do it alone, cold turkey?"

"Cold turkey," the elder Jenson replied. "I think it's much better for you to sell yourself up front; then your clients won't have any preconceived ideas about you or your ability to handle their accounts. Good luck. We'll see you at nine o'clock in the morning."

The two Jensons left the office. After a quick perusal of the file cabinet that housed the inherited accounts, Tyler closed the office door and walked down the hall to give Diane, his assigned account assistant, his home phone number and address. Diane was a large redhead who, from all outward appearances, had lived a rather fast, hard life. She fit in the category of "wide-bodied" in the jet set, descriptive world of trendy people. When Tyler arrived at her desk she looked up and said, with obvious annoyance, "Yes?"

Right away, Tyler could tell that he didn't care much for this woman. Just who in the hell does she think she is? he thought. "I want to leave you my phone number and address just in case someone needs to contact me. I haven't been in town long, and I haven't had time to call anyone."

Diane never looked up from her work. "Jot it down here, on this memo pad. I'll put it in the office circular when I get time. Never enough time around here to take care of all the work that has to be done, much less this menial crap."

Tyler quickly scribbled down his phone number and address, left the office, and headed for a little pub he had noticed when returning from lunch. Entering the pub, Tyler quickly glanced around the room at the after-work crowd that had assembled. These people had come to rinse from their minds events that had created mental cobwebs after working a long day in the stressful environment of Chicago's financial world.

Tyler selected an empty barstool about two-thirds of the way down the bar and sat down to enjoy a double shot of his favorite. He called out, "Bourbon and soda, with a twist of lemon."

The bartender, a short, bald, docile-looking man in his mid-sixties, poured the drink and slid it across the bar in a single motion, demonstrating that he had done this no less than a few thousand times. "That'll be $3.50," he said in a bored, monotonous voice. "We take American Express, Visa, and MasterCard. No personal checks."

Tyler reached for his money clip and meticulously pulled out a twenty-dollar bill, laying it in front of the newly acquired, spirit-enhanced liquid.

"Wanna run a tab?" the bartender asked.

"No, just take it out of this."

Tyler shoved the twenty closer to the elderly gentleman, who took it and turned to get Tyler's change. The first sip of whiskey flooded Tyler's mouth and made him shiver. Swallowing it was difficult. He always responded this way to the first taste, but every sip thereafter was smoother and easier to get down.

Tyler finished the drink and ordered another, feeling a little celebration was appropriate. "New job, new city, new boss, new home—there were several reasons he had to justify a second bourbon. The bar had settled down. The local patrons were sipping their drinks, jabbering away, and smoking their long-due cigarettes after a day in their smoke-free work environments.

"Name's Sid," the bartender said as he moved Tyler's drink to wipe the badly worn hardwood bar.

"Tyler Trenton." Tyler reached to shake the hand of his new acquaintance.

"Haven't seen you in here before," the bartender said. "Work around here?"

"I'm new in town, and associated with the Jenson and Jenson firm down the street," Tyler responded.

"Oh, yes," Sid said. "Several of the guys and a couple of the gals come here from time to time. Welcome to Chicago—not a bad town. It kind of gets in your blood. It's hard to leave, you know."

"That's what I hear," Tyler responded. "Never been in your fair city until two weeks ago. I'm anxious to get my roots down and check the place out."

Sid was beckoned down the bar and left to fetch another Budweiser for a neatly attired young man and the woman sitting next to him. Tyler finished his second drink, tossed down two one-dollar bills for the tip, and got up to leave. Sid had suddenly gotten very busy pouring seconds.

"Come back soon, and take care of yourself," Tyler heard as he passed through the door which led outside.

The late fall evening was chilly, damp, and typically breezy from the air moving in off the lake. Tyler had walked to work, as finding a place to park was difficult in the downtown area. Besides, he only lived a short distance from his office. The exercise was good for him, as was the crisp, fresh air that filled his lungs during his brisk walk home.

Chapter Three

The rest of the month was largely a get-acquainted period for Tyler, marked by frequent trips to clients' offices and long periods of waiting for appointments. Brokers are normally not a top priority on the list of people to see in the routine day of most high-salary executives. Typically, investors only want to hear from their portfolio managers when the news is good, or when a "gut-cinch" tip is available. However, initial acquaintances needed to be made in person, after which the phone would likely be the means of contact.

By the end of the first month, Tyler's commissions had far exceeded his expectations. After taxes, he had earned nearly four thousand dollars, due to the efforts of his predecessor and a few good "hits" he had made on his own in the volatile futures market—not bad, and much better than he had hoped for during his breaking-in period.

Tyler folded his paycheck, stub detached, and placed it in the breast pocket of his suit coat. Before departing the office, he left word with Diane that he wouldn't be back for the rest of the day. He walked to the bank and deposited his check, keeping a few hundred dollars in cash for spending money, then stopped by the pub for a little bourbon and soda.

It was a little early for the work crowd, and Tyler found Sid sitting on the end barstool, stirring a cup of coffee and reading the evening *Tribune*.

"Sid," Tyler said, and slid up on the stool next to him. "Kind of slow today?"

"Not really," Sid responded. "Just relaxing a little before the 'schizos' get off work and come charging in for their 'unwinds,' filling the place with their bullshit stories about how they are overworked and underpaid. Same old consistent flow of bullshit, day in and day out. I must like it though, or I would leave this smoke-filled joint and get a real job."

Sid slid off the stool, walked behind the bar, and reached for Tyler's standard. "Same medicine as always?" he asked.

"Yeah, better have one. I certainly don't want to make anyone think I come in here to visit with you. Might impair my ability to make any friends."

Sid grinned his usual "feel-like-I-have-to" grin and poured the bourbon over some ice that he had scooped from the stainless steel tub.

The bar was starting to fill when Tyler finished his drink and set the empty glass on the tip tray at the back of the bar. "One more, then cut me off," he said to Sid.

"What about me?" Tyler half turned to see Brenda, who had approached him from the back. He had met her before on several occasions in his drinking career at the newfound pub.

"Hi, kid," Tyler responded. "I guess I could buy you a drink. Sit down here and tell me about life in the fast lane."

Brenda removed her trench coat and carefully placed it over a barstool, then slid up and sat on top of it. "Great to see you again, Tyler. Thought I may have run you off the other night. I wasn't expecting to see you for a while," Brenda said.

"Well, you did reveal your 'true blonde' attitude the other night. You should cool it when you drink, or someone might think you are an easy lady," Tyler responded.

"God, did I act that bad the other night?" Brenda asked. "If I offended you, please forgive me. I had a bad day."

Tyler grinned and said, "No offense taken; it just seemed kind of out of character for you." Tyler quickly changed the subject, commenting on the weather—a quick fix for any conversation that becomes uncomfortable.

Brenda was an attractive blonde lady in her mid-thirties, but she presented all the characteristics of a pampered, mid-twenty-year-old woman. She had exquisite taste in clothing and jewelry, and she was always very fresh-looking, with her natural blonde hair brushed back on one side. Brenda had blue eyes, thick lips, and a nice figure. She could certainly pick her gentleman escorts from the more elite group wherever she might be. Unfortunately, she had been in an automobile accident that had left her with a rather ugly V-shaped scar above her left eyebrow, which made her extremely self-conscious.

She often rubbed that eyebrow nervously, attempting to cover the scar or erase it from existence.

She had graduated from a small college in Iowa and moved to Chicago to pursue a career in the garment industry. Selling women's sporting apparel was her endeavor, and she was quite successful in her marketing career with an expensive, trendy company named Foxy Fabrics, a locally owned manufacturing and marketing firm that sold their merchandise to a few quality department store chains and select specialty shops. Brenda's career required a lot of travel, making any kind of long-term relationship nearly impossible. She was very easy to talk to, definitely projecting the qualities of honesty and trustworthiness. Tyler liked Brenda, and probably could have been convinced to give a relationship with her a whirl, but he just wasn't ready for romance. His life had settled down some, and he was enjoying it immensely.

Brenda finished her glass of Zinfandel and turned to Tyler. "Want to go grab a sandwich?"

"Sure," Tyler said, sliding off the stool and helping Brenda with her coat. They discussed the options and settled on going to a small Italian deli around the corner.

Brenda and Tyler walked slowly to the deli and selected a small table near the back. The room was divided by a small walk-up bar in the middle. It was a cozy little place with red and white checkered oilcloth covering the tables and wrought-iron chairs. The deli was dimly lit and charming, and was noted for its great food.

Tyler ordered a hot pastrami on rye with a pickle, and Brenda selected the Italian meatball sandwich on sourdough bread. They each ordered a glass of the house wine and a small dinner salad as well.

Their conversation that evening went the entire circle, from Tyler's broken marriage to Brenda's short-lived experience as a cocktail waitress in the small town where she had attended college. Brenda was an interesting person, and was well-read on current as well as historical world events. She even had some limited knowledge of Tyler's line of work as an investment broker. Tyler soon realized that Brenda was a knowledgeable, neat young lady.

Tyler and Brenda ended the evening with a relaxing stroll through the art museum. After a tender hug and a kiss on the cheek, Tyler put Brenda in a taxi, flipped the driver a ten-dollar bill, and headed back to his townhouse, where he soon fell asleep.

When Tyler awakened early the next morning, he lay in bed with his hands cupped behind his head and stared at the ceiling. A lot had happened to him in his short life. He reminisced about his time as a football player, and wondered how his career would have been in the NFL had he not been injured. It was almost as though he could hear the cheer of the crowd and the loudspeaker in the background announcing his name: "The tackle was made by Trenton—Tyler Trenton. Loss of two yards on the play. Third down." Tyler's first love in the whole world was football, and he missed the game and the recognition that went along with playing it.

If only—if, if, if, Tyler thought. It wasn't meant to be . . . I've got to get on with my life. I'll work my ass off for the prestige I want. I can do it right where I am. Jenson and Jenson can provide me with the money to have a respectable lifestyle, and I'll get the recognition I want.

Tyler crawled out of bed and headed for the shower.

Chapter Four

Every Monday morning, the Jenson brothers held a staff meeting. This was intended to give account managers an opportunity to share their portfolio successes or failures with the two Jensons and the other account managers. Participation was mandatory, and absence was not taken lightly by the Jensons, or by the staff members. The Jensons' meeting quickly acquired a pet name—"the sweat-pit." Everyone anticipated it with dread. "The pit" was a terrible way to start the week. It normally took the rest of the day to get back into "aggressive pursuit" mode, so Mondays were essentially a lost day. Other than the regular sweat-pit, life at the firm was enjoyable and extremely profitable. The Jensons' brokerage enjoyed a reputation in the financial district as a firm that could always find a way to earn an above-average return on investment. The brothers didn't meddle with their managers and seldom even talked to them, unless, of course, clients called and complained. Their relationship with their managers was casual but firm, providing a work environment that was respected by every employee.

With his numerous successes and a growing list of affluent clientele, Tyler was soon promoted to vice-president and senior account manager for the firm. He was good, and the word spread quickly among the investors, who were constantly looking for help with their portfolios.

Along with his prestigious title came added responsibility. Tyler was expected to do more entertaining and spend longer hours coaching the junior account managers. He gained the added responsibility of directing the activities and discussions in the sweat-pit, which he hated. This was not Tyler's cup of tea, and he struggled with it. He soon found it was hard to get up on Monday morning, knowing he had to face the agonizing faces of the bored attendees. They used to be his friends and associates, but now they looked at him like army recruits who had just been informed that they had been selected to clean the mess hall grease trap.

It was late in the day when the phone rang. Tyler picked it up on the second ring. "Tyler," he said into the receiver.

"Tyler, this is Brenda. How have you been?"

"Working. All I do is work," Tyler said. "How about you?"

"Oh, same old thing. I just returned to town from a boring trip to Salt Lake City, Utah. I had a terrible trip—seventeen inches of snow, and I had to spend three entire days in a motel with a terrible restaurant and a broken television set. The only thing that could have made it worse would be to have diarrhea and two broken arms at the same time. God, it's great to be home." She sighed, then continued. "Want to meet for a drink and maybe dinner?"

"Great idea," Tyler remarked. "Time and place—you name it."

"How about if you come to my place?" Brenda asked. "I have some great wine, and I'll stop and pick up some Chinese food. I'll see you whenever you get there. I should be home by six." Tyler hung up, shoved a small pile of unfinished paperwork into his top drawer, switched the phone to the night mode, and left the office. He was anxious to see Brenda. He enjoyed her exuberance for life and her relentless energy.

Along the way, Tyler stopped in front of his office building to pick out a small bouquet of mixed, sweet-smelling flowers. Brenda loved flowers, and treated them like small, helpless children. She would talk to them and water them daily, attempting to prolong their life and enjoying every single moment of their existence. Often, a small tear would form and slowly work its way down her cheek when the time finally came to relinquish them to the trash receptacle. Brenda was a very loving and caring person whose feelings were easily hurt. Tyler would do his best to be kind to her.

Tyler went home and showered. He selected a casual pair of pleated denim trousers, a navy, wool, V-neck sweater, and a pair of Adidas tennis shoes. Throwing on his leather World War II bomber jacket, he grabbed the flowers and headed to Brenda's place.

When Brenda opened the door Tyler noted that she was casually dressed in a pair of white jersey sweat pants and a loose-fitting pink sweat shirt. Her hair was beautiful, as usual. Tyler couldn't help but notice the firm protrusions under her sweat shirt. She obviously hadn't bothered to put on a bra. Nice touch.

Brenda greeted him with an affectionate little hug, after which she pulled back to look at a face she hadn't seen for a while. "Great to see you, Tyler. I've really missed you." Tyler pulled off his coat and turned to search for a place to put it. "Here, I'll hang it in the hall closet. Give it to me," Brenda said.

"Thanks," Tyler responded as he headed to one of the two woven-bamboo barstools by the bar that divided the kitchen and small dining room.

"Glass of wine?" Brenda offered.

"Got anything a little stronger?" Tyler asked.

"Sure, over here, under the counter. Come pick out what you want. I don't think you'll find any bourbon. I wanted to pick up a bottle for you, but didn't think of it when I went to the liquor store."

Tyler opened the cabinet door and examined the few bottles stored inside. He selected a sealed bottle of Makers Mark; he had tried it before and found it tasteful and smooth.

"This will do. Moochers can't be too particular, huh?" He ran his fingernail around the groove in the bottleneck just below the cap to cut the red wax seal, which provided a touch of uniqueness to the square-shaped bottle. He poured about three fingers of the dark liquid into a glass and threw in four large ice cubes from the ice bucket.

Brenda had already poured herself a glass of white wine, and she held the glass up. "*Salud*," she said, clicking her wineglass against the glass of bourbon in Tyler's hand. He winked at her and said, "Here's looking at ya," and each of them sipped a little of the liquid from their glasses.

The entire evening was relaxing and enjoyable for both of them. After eating the Chinese food that Brenda had brought home, they retired to the couch and sleepily watched the tail end of the Seton Hall-Georgetown game. As usual, the game was close, with the Georgetown Hoyas the victors.

"John Thompson prevails again," Tyler said, and pushed the remote button to peruse the rest of the channels for something interesting to watch.

By this time Brenda had laid her head in Tyler's lap and lay looking straight up at his face. "Tyler, why don't you come with me next month?"

"Where are you headed?" Tyler asked.

"Believe it or not, I am headed to wonderful Wyoming. Ever been there? Or do you even know where it is?"

Tyler looked down at Brenda. "Sure, I've been there. It's a neat place."

"Jackson, Wyoming—Jackson Hole is its real name. Tyler, it's the most beautiful place in the world. Huge pine-covered mountains accented with snow, and in the summer the green meadows are utterly breathtaking. Please come with me!"

Tyler hesitated to respond, as the idea held no interest for him. He smiled and passively said, "I'll think about it."

By the tone of his voice, Brenda could tell that Tyler was as excited about going to Wyoming as he was about attending the sweat-pit on Monday mornings. "Honest, Tyler, the wildlife is every-where. We probably couldn't get up to Yellowstone National Park this time of year to see Old Faithful, but Jackson is a hoot. I have to help one of our new specialty distributors set up some merchandis-ing displays and go over our spring order program. It'll probably take a day, no longer. Then, we could take the weekend to cruise around Jackson Hole, and maybe even get in some skiing. Please?"

Tyler again responded, "I'll think about it; I promise I will."

He turned his face from the television to look at Brenda. With the sparkle in her eye and the eager look of anticipation on her soft, pretty face, Tyler couldn't help thinking how perfect she would look if it weren't for the scar near her eye. She was really beautiful. Tyler bent down and kissed her forehead. Brenda reached up, grabbed his cheeks between her hands, and placed her soft, moist mouth over his. It was heaven. Tyler softly closed his eyes, his head spinning in ecstasy. The kiss was warm and sweet. Tyler wanted it to never end. Finally, he lifted his head and pulled away from her trembling lips. "That was sweet, Brenda."

Brenda smiled, then slowly turned her head to gaze at the tele-vision as if she had something to say, but just couldn't find the words. She lay there for several minutes, her little finger resting on the corner of her mouth. She did have something to say, but she didn't know how, or where to start. She finally raised herself up and pecked him on the cheek.

"Guess I should go," Tyler said. He stood and started toward the hall closet to retrieve his coat. Brenda walked toward the kitchen and leaned against the divider, waiting for him to return. Tyler pulled on his coat and came up behind her, put his arms around her waist, and leaned down to gently kiss her on the ear. Brenda shrugged her shoulders and pressed her trembling body against Tyler as close as she could. Not a word was spoken; the couple stood in silence. The embrace lasted several minutes. Finally, Tyler backed away and walked to the door. Brenda heard the door open and close behind him.

The next day was busy for Tyler. The market had been soft, and clients were getting nervous. He received several more phone calls than usual, and didn't even have time for lunch. At three o'clock, the New York Exchange closed down for the day and things got quiet—a welcome change of pace for Tyler.

The next few days at work were much the same. Tyler could feel himself starting to get a little testy with the continual pressures that accompanied the market fluctuations. The phone calls were rampant, as nervous clients called to minimize their losses with orders to sell. The Dow Jones was dropping, and the managed portfolios were disappearing like alley crapshooters in a police raid. This went on through Thursday, and on Friday the market finally started to stabilize. The Dow settled around lunch time, and by closing it had picked up two and three-quarter points. By Monday it was apparent that the slump was over, as the Dow picked up another four and a half points. By two o'clock on Tuesday afternoon, most of the portfolios were back in the files, and things returned to normal.

Tyler needed a break. He decided to get away for a few days. Remembering Brenda's offer, he reluctantly picked up the phone to give her a call. Tyler had never wanted to go to Wyoming, but going any place with Brenda would be a nice change of pace. To be honest, a damp, cold, empty feeling came over him when he thought of her going without him.

She wouldn't dare, he thought, knowing deep down that she probably would.

Chapter

Five

The plane ride from Chicago to Salt Lake City took about two hours and forty-five minutes. After a forty-five minute layover, Brenda and Tyler were on their way to Jackson Hole, Wyoming. When the plane dropped through the cloud cover, the mountains suddenly sprung up to meet them. It looked as though the plane was headed directly into a wall of snow-covered mountains, but then the plane turned sharply to the left and continued its descent. The wheels touched the ground, and the engines sounded as though they would explode when the pilot put them into reverse thrust to aid the deceleration on the runway, which was much too short. The plane turned sharply at a speed which seemed unusually fast, and the passengers were bounced around as the wheels crossed over a crack in the concrete. The Boeing 727-200 taxied up to the small, busy airport and finally stopped.

Tyler looked over at Brenda. "Had me wondering for a while. They should stretch this runway out another half mile or so."

Brenda smiled. "I've been here twice before, and it was that way both times. I think it's exciting, don't you?"

"It's not my idea of fun," Tyler responded.

The walk from the airplane was breathtakingly cold. Tyler hadn't dressed warmly enough for this weather. The temperature was near zero, and there was a stiff breeze blowing from the southwest. A skiff of snow blanketed the concrete landing mat which led to the terminal door. Inside, the terminal was packed with passengers who waited impatiently for their luggage to arrive on the single carousel, already full of yet-unclaimed duffel bags, suitcases, and bulky ski equipment.

Tyler twisted and turned his way through the waves of tourists and skiers who were busy talking and planning. Finally, he reached the car rental counter and presented his driver's license and credit card to the agent, who obviously needed a day or two off to adjust her rude, angry attitude. After about ten minutes of observing the disorganized, highly frustrated agent shuffling paper and pecking on the computer keyboard, a car rental agreement was shoved under Tyler's nose for the usual initialing and signature. The agent dug through an old cigar box full of car keys, studied the metal-rimmed tag on one set, and tossed them up on the counter.

"Space eleven, out that door, white Jeep Cherokee. And be sure to return the car with the tank full, or we'll have to charge you $2.50 a gallon." Tyler grabbed the keys and shoved the sloppy, creased contract into his jacket pocket, then left the counter.

Brenda had dragged their luggage into a corner and was casually sitting on a large wooden crate that housed what appeared to be something like a large pump.

"Ready at last," Tyler remarked as he reached to pick up the two larger suitcases. "Can you get that little one? I'll get these two big hummers."

Tyler led the way to the lot, opened the rear door to the Cherokee, placed the three pieces of luggage inside, and slammed the door. The engine of the Cherokee groaned as he turned the key in the ignition. After a few tries it fired and started. The Cherokee had obviously seen better days, but Tyler felt lucky to have even gotten a car, considering the condition that the agent was in when he rented it. After warming the engine for a few minutes, he placed the vehicle in reverse. Creaking and groaning, the stubborn tires began to move, and the Cherokee backed out from the parking space.

The trip to Jackson took about thirty minutes, as traffic was moving very slowly on the snow-packed road. There was plenty of time to observe the huge elk feeding ground on the left of the road. Two or three thousand elk could be seen, some of them lying down to digest the hay that the Game and Fish Department fed them daily, and some standing around in tightknit little groups to share their warmth. Tyler had read about the feeding ground in the travel magazine located in the seat pocket on the airplane. The article explained its operation and told how the herd migrated there every winter to be fed by the Game and Fish Department. The department spent many thousands of dollars annually to feed the animals. The elk arrived every year, migrating to the huge feeding grounds, seeking safety in the posted game reserve from the relentless hunters' bullets. The huge bulls were majestic, their heavily antlered heads held high as if to project an image of being immortal. The magazine couldn't begin to describe how beautiful the elk were, or to enable a person to understand what two or three thousand elk look like in one gigantic herd. It was simply incredible. Incredible.

Tyler pulled the Cherokee into the parking lot of the quaint, Western-looking lodge where Brenda had made a reservation. Once inside, the atmosphere changed dramatically. The huge lobby in the lodge was finished in what appeared to be natural logs. The vaulted ceiling provided lots of wall space, which was adorned with several magnificent mounted elk, deer, and antelope heads. On the far end of the lobby was a huge natural-stone fireplace in which several large logs burned lazily, providing an atmosphere that was charming and warm. Along the outside wall of the lobby was a long bar where a dozen or so patrons sat, sipping their drinks. All were dressed in Levi's, boots, Western shirts, and cowboy hats—either natives, or quickly converted tourists. Tyler felt a little out of place in his Dockers, button-down sports shirt, and leather topsiders.

Tyler and Brenda checked into a room on the second floor, up a wooden staircase that went halfway to the landing, then turned to the other direction to complete the journey. The room, though a little on the small side, had been tastefully decorated like a ranch house, with one bed covered by a colorful Indian-blanket-design, down-filled comforter.

How cozy and romantic, Brenda thought as she examined the bathroom and checked out the small closet in the corner. She turned to face Tyler and asked, "Isn't this a great room? I've stayed in this room before. I enjoyed it so much that I asked for it again when I called for the reservation."

"I like it," Tyler said, straining his eyes so he could see to adjust the thermostat on the wall. "Let's unload our bags and go down for a toddy. I could use one."

Brenda unloaded her bag and hung her clothes in the closet, then carefully placed the rest in a dresser drawer. Tyler also unloaded his bag, putting all his clothing in the remaining drawers of the dresser. He placed the emptied suitcase on the floor and scooted it under the bed with his toe.

The cozy bar was buzzing with chatter as Brenda and Tyler entered. They studied the area closely and selected a small table near the fireplace. The fire cracked lazily, providing a warm, sleepy environment with its radiant heat.

Tyler pulled the chair out for Brenda, then pulled his own chair as close to hers as he could. "What sounds good to you?" he asked.

Brenda stared into the fire and said, "I think I'll have a daiquiri. Strawberry sounds good to me."

The cocktail waitress, attired in Western-style clothing, came over and placed a napkin in front of each of them. "Draft beer is a dollar, and well drinks two dollars, until six," she announced.

Tyler placed their order, then leaned back in the chair and stretched, his arms extended high in the air. "I kind of dig this place," he said. "But I need to do some unwinding to get into the flow of things. Things move a little slower around here."

The drinks went down smooth, and in fact, in Brenda's terminology, they had a "more-ish" taste, so they had more. After their third drink, the tired travelers began to loosen up and relax. In fact, Brenda was getting kind of cuddly and warm. She placed her arm on Tyler's shoulder and leaned forward to kiss him on the ear.

"I think I'll go shower before dinner," she whispered. "Want to come?"

Tyler took her hand and squeezed it gently. "Sure, I could use one myself. If I don't move around I'll probably fall asleep right here in this chair."

Once upstairs, Tyler placed the key in the lock and shoved the door open so Brenda could enter. Inside, he closed the door, secured the deadbolt, and tossed the room key onto the small desk beside the door.

Brenda immediately began to remove her clothing. Tyler walked over to the window, parted the curtains, and gazed at the street below, not wanting to make Brenda feel like she was on stage. She tossed the last of her undergarments onto the bed and walked directly into Tyler's arms as he turned to face her. Their lips met. The kiss was warm and passionate, and Brenda squirmed sweetly in Tyler's arms. They stood there for some time embracing each other, Tyler gently moving his fingertips up and down Brenda's spine.

Brenda slowly pulled away and said, "I think I'd better get in the shower, or we might miss dinner." She walked into the bathroom and closed the door.

Tyler moved away from the window and turned on the television. As in most remote Western towns, the viewing choice was somewhat limited. He settled for the evening news and stared at the screen as the commentator discussed the events of the day.

Dinner at a nearby restaurant that evening was delightful. Tyler enjoyed one of the best steaks he had ever eaten, with baked beans and a large baked potato. The bottle of dry wine that he selected proved to be quite a compatible choice. They finished dinner and planned their stay while finishing the last of the wine.

The trip back to the hotel was short, and the time required to crawl in the comfortable bed was minimal. They fell asleep quickly, tired from the long day of travel, the great dinner, and the wine. The two of them slept comfortably that night, tangled and cozy under the down-filled comforter.

Chapter Six

Tyler woke early to the sound of the shower. Brenda had gotten up and was preparing to go to the dress shop to get her work completed so she and Tyler could spend the weekend together. Tyler lay in the bed, enjoying the feeling of not having to go to work. It was great. In fact, he might just stay in bed all morning. He rolled over and pulled the covers over his head, sinking into a deep slumber.

Tyler woke again later in the morning and strained to see his watch in the dimly lit room. The dial read 9:27, and he was still in bed. This had to be some kind of a record. He would have to go back a long way in his life to remember a day when he had slept this late. Rested and hungry, Tyler threw back the blankets, climbed from bed, and lazily got into the shower. The water was refreshing, splashing off his face and bringing life to his body. He was now ready to face the world.

The sun was shining as Tyler left the hotel, after a delicious breakfast, to explore the little Western town. He walked for about ten minutes before wandering into a tastefully decorated art gallery. Original works of many of the local artists were displayed on the walls, and some of the nicer and more expensive ones were displayed on easels around the room. Most of the work appeared to be of local scenery and wildlife. He started his tour with the art by the entrance and studied each framed masterpiece, casually strolling through the gallery. He noticed the artists' names, many of which he recognized.

Tyler stopped to study one painting that had caught his eye. It portrayed a fawn lying in a bed of colorful fallen leaves and surrounded by Indian paintbrushes, the Wyoming state flower. The scene was completed with a stand of colorful aspens and mountains in the background, and the contrast of the colors of the beautiful blue sky, the Indian paintbrushes, and the aspen trees was gorgeous. Tyler turned the price tag over–$350. Not bad. It would look great in his office. He purchased the framed painting and arranged to have it shipped to Chicago. He got a brief history of the artist, where she lived, and an overview of some of her other works as the clerk took down his address and billed the cost to his credit card.

Tyler spent the rest of the morning wandering through gift shops and other art galleries. At lunch time he found a small, quaint restaurant named "Rustlers Roost." It was crowded with Western-attired folks who made him feel quite welcome, even though he looked for all the world like a slick Chicago guy. Tyler had to change that if he was going to stay for a few days. Perhaps he could purchase some Levi's and boots, and maybe even a cowboy hat. That would be fun.

After lunch, Tyler did just that. He found a Western store and began trying on boots. He eventually picked out a of nice brown pair with what the clerk called "roper heels"—heels that were not too tall and were larger in diameter than the traditional cowboy boot heel. Next, he was fitted with a pair of Levi's, selecting ones that had the appearance of being worn and laundered many times before. He picked out a jacket to match. He also selected a blue-gray plaid Western-cut shirt with pearl-colored snap buttons and a Western belt of tooled leather, about the same color as the boots. To complete the outfit, Tyler chose a brown felt Western hat with a braided leather band. He decided to wear his newly acquired clothing and put his Chicago casuals in the large bag provided by the store. He felt like a real Western dude.

The day was warm, and the remaining piles of snow were slowly melting and running in small streams from the sidewalk into the street. Tyler walked back to the hotel and found Brenda in their room.

"Wow!" she exclaimed as Tyler entered. "You look like you belong here!"

Tyler grinned, grasped his jacket lapels with both hands, and cocked his head to the side, turning in a complete circle. "Native, strictly native," he said. "Amazing what you can buy for five hundred dollars in Jackson."

"I love it," Brenda said. "I want some boots, too. Can we go get some?"

The clerk looked up in surprise as Tyler and Brenda entered the store. "We need another cowboy outfit," Tyler said. Brenda was already sorting through the boots that lined one complete wall of the store. She selected a pair of dark brown leather boots, also with roper heels. Soon she too was fully outfitted, with boots, Levi's, a Western-cut blouse, a belt, and a tan suede hat with a colorful beaded band. In no time, Tyler had spent another five hundred dollars. Then, the two visitors looked like locals, ready to mix with the natives.

They strolled around the city, visiting some of the gift shops and galleries that Tyler had enjoyed, stopping at the gallery where he had purchased the painting along the way. Tyler was anxious for Brenda to see it. She loved it as much as Tyler did.

After a leisurely dinner, the couple found themselves in a night-club where a cowboy band was playing. "Long necks" (bottled beers) appeared to be the drink of the evening, so they ordered a couple. The band was loud, and the dance floor was crazy with "shit-kick-ers," as the natives called them. Brenda and Tyler had to try it. They felt embarrassingly awkward during the first couple of songs, then got into the swing of it. They danced and drank, danced and drank. The new dancing style was great, but their feet were killing them. The boots were definitely the accepted style, but Brenda and Tyler had to stop before they could no longer walk.

They headed back for the hotel. Sleep came easily and quickly that night.

The next day was beautiful. Brenda and Tyler got into their rented Cherokee to drive to the mountains. The temperature was already up to fifty-seven degrees, as reported on the car radio, and it was just past nine o'clock. They had somehow gotten their aching, sore feet back into the cowboy boots. Looking very Western, they pulled out of the parking lot and headed south along the Snake River. They spent the day exploring the mountains, walking along clear, bubbling, spring-fed creeks. At one point they stumbled onto a fawn bedded down in a small clump of aspens. The startled fawn jumped up and quickly disappeared into the heavy underbrush by the creek that meandered down the mountainside. The painting that Tyler had purchased now took on an entirely different mean-ing for them. Tyler loved this place, and Brenda was happy.

It was approaching evening when they returned. Tyler was exu-berant, thrilled by the Wyoming mountains. Why hadn't he discov-ered them before? The tranquillity, the color, and the fresh crisp air, not to mention the noticeable lack of people, brought great beauty to this lonely, peaceful place. The sky was much bluer here than

Tyler had ever seen it. The well-kept secret of Wyoming's beauty was now a part of Tyler. He would be back.

The following day was another beauty. They had arranged for a horseback ride in the mountains, and brought a sack lunch of cold roast beef sandwiches, chips, and cookies. Food had never tasted so good. What was it about this newly discovered paradise that Tyler loved so much? Was Wyoming really that great, or was it Brenda's presence that Tyler so enjoyed? Whatever it was, Tyler wanted it to last. Brenda, too, was happy, infatuated with this gorgeous place. Or was it Tyler that made it so beautiful? Things were going well for Brenda and Tyler. Brenda was clearly developing intimate feelings for Tyler. It wasn't like she saw sparklers or heard firecrackers when she closed her eyes; it was more like a warm, comfortable feeling that made her feel very secure and a little tingly, like someone running their tongue around the outside edge of her ear.

Tomorrow was D day, the day they must depart the new land that they had in such a short time learned to enjoy. It was a sad day for both of them. They arose from their deep slumber wrapped around one another, just as they had been when sleep overtook their tired bodies the previous evening. Brenda and Tyler had managed to work a lot of activity into a short period of time.

Packing their suitcases was painful. Neither of them wanted to leave. But, as with all good things, this too had to come to an end. Tyler patted Brenda on the back and announced that he was going down to check out. Quickly clearing the hotel account, Tyler wandered into the hotel gift shop. After examining several books on the shelf, he selected two to take home with him. One was titled *Wyoming in Detail*, and the other, *Wilderness at Its Best*. Tyler returned to the room and shoved the books into his duffel. He wanted to know more about this mysterious state. With all its natural beauty, why was it so sparsely populated?

Brenda finished packing, and they headed down the stairs for the trip to the airport. Tyler was quiet along the way, constantly gazing out the Cherokee's windows at the mountains, painting his mind with their beauty. He wanted to remember every single rock and tree.

After their luggage was checked, the two travelers headed down to the loading gate. The passengers had already started boarding the plane. Tyler and Brenda handed their ticket folders to the agent and passed through the door.

The short flight to Salt Lake City was uneventful. The flight from Salt Lake to Chicago left on time, and would have them home in about two hours and forty minutes. Tyler gazed out the window as the plane taxied into takeoff position.

Tyler closed his eyes and drifted into sleep. He dreamed of being a small boy, of the fun that he had as a child. His grandfather was a good friend, often taking him to the woods on camping trips, where they would fish and swim in the creeks. Tyler loved that. He remembered how he enjoyed sleeping in the tent, and how neat it was when it rained, how well he slept as the drops peppered the tent in their soothing rhythm. He remembered how warm and safe he felt in his sleeping bag with his little dog Buffy curled up tightly against him. He remembered the campfires, how everyone would sit around in the evening, gazing into the flames as they warmed their bodies, and the mesmerized stares on their faces as they sat around like cigar-store Indians. Tyler had loved the outdoors as a child, and wondered why he never took the time to enjoy it as an adult. He realized that he had missed it immensely.

It was 10:15 at night when Tyler arrived back at his townhouse. He slowly unpacked his duffel, putting most of the clothes back in their respective places. Most of them had not been worn. The new Western clothes were another story. They were badly soiled, and went into the laundry hamper. He picked up his boots and brushed them off with a dirty sock, then proudly placed them in the bottom of his closet. He returned the duffel bag to the closet shelf, then placed the two books he had purchased on the night stand by his bed. Tyler was looking forward to reading them. He wanted to learn more about the land he had just visited.

Tyler crawled into the shower before retiring for the evening. He was about to doze off for the night when the phone rang. It was Brenda.

"Did you get unpacked okay?"

"Yes, I did," he responded.

"Tyler, I just wanted to tell you what a great time I had, and how much I enjoyed having you with me. The trip just wouldn't have been the same without you."

"Wouldn't have missed it for the world, Brenda," Tyler responded. "Sleep well, honey, and I'll talk to you tomorrow. Tomorrow is a workday, you know."

"Good night Tyler, and sweet dreams." Brenda ended the conversation with a smacking sound, as if she were giving him a kiss, and hung up the phone.

A smile came across Tyler's face as he thought, What a sweetheart she is. He turned out the lamp on the night stand and rolled over, drifting into dreamland. He slept well, but missed his little snuggling buddy a lot.

That night Tyler dreamed of Wyoming and its beauty, a beauty that was now deeply entrenched in his heart and mind.

Chapter Seven

Tyler arrived at work early and quickly shuffled through the piles of documents that had accumulated on his desk in his absence. Monday was sweat-pit day, and Tyler wanted to catch up on what had happened while he was gone. Discovering that things looked pretty much the same as when he had left, he headed for the conference room, where most of the attendees had already gathered, sipping coffee and making small talk.

After the long and tortuous meeting, Tyler returned to his office to handle the remainder of the paperwork on his desk. It was a busy day. At one point, he took a few moments to check the status of his personal investment portfolio. It was doing well. It gave him a feeling of satisfaction to see how large the cash value of his investments had grown. He was rapidly approaching financial freedom. Retirement at forty? he thought. Possibly, if the market didn't completely go to hell. He quietly made a fist and shook it firmly, as if to say, "Give 'em hell, Tyler." Startled, Tyler turned his head to see Mr. Jenson in the doorway of his office.

"May I come in?" Mr. Jenson entered the office and walked over to one of Tyler's guest chairs, sat down, and leaned back cautiously before proceeding. "Tyler, you are a good man. I have been watching you with a lot of interest. You are a godsend to our organization. I just wanted to let you know that your efforts aren't going unnoticed. We would really miss you if you were to leave us."

Tyler walked over and sat down in the overstuffed chair behind his desk, puzzled by Mr. Jenson's comment. "Thank you, Mr. Jenson. I wasn't expecting that, and don't quite know what to say."

"You don't have to say anything, Tyler. I just wanted you to know."

Mr. Jenson got up from the chair and departed the room as suddenly as he had entered. I wonder what that was all about, Tyler thought. Old fart must be feeling guilty about something, or else he's getting ready to bust my balls for some reason.

Only a few minutes later, Tyler was startled by a crystal-shattering scream coming from down the hall. He ran to the door, where he encountered Mr. Jenson's private secretary. "It's Mr. Jenson, he's collapsed! Call the ambulance! Quick, down here, in his office!"

Tyler pushed his way through the small crowd to Mr. Jenson's office, where he found the man slumped over his desk. He rushed over and placed his fingers on the man's neck, nervously attempting to find a pulse. There was none. Mr. Jenson had merely laid his head down on his desk and died. Tyler backed away, walked to the door, and turned to look back at Mr. Jenson's lifeless body. He quietly closed the door.

"He's gone," Tyler announced to the shocked audience that had gathered.

Tyler went back to his office and waited for the paramedics to arrive. Twenty minutes later, he saw the sheet-covered body being carted down the hall and into the waiting elevator.

Soon afterward, the other Jenson entered Tyler's office with reddened eyes, disheveled and obviously in shock. Tyler took his arm and guided him to the chair in front of his desk.

"Here, sit here, Mr. Jenson. I'm dreadfully sorry about your brother. I can't believe it. He was just in my office a few minutes ago. Terrible loss. I just can't believe it."

Mr. Jenson shook his head in disbelief and reached for his handkerchief to blot the tears from his eyes. He just sat there, staring at the floor. After several minutes of silence, the old man rose.

"Can I see you home, Mr. Jenson?" Tyler asked.

"That would be nice, Tyler. I don't know if I'm up to driving. I hate to be burdensome, but I would really appreciate it if you would drive me home."

Tyler slipped on his coat, closed his briefcase, and walked Mr. Jenson to the elevator. He took the car keys from Mr. Jenson's trembling hand and carefully helped the shaken man into the car. Arriving at his home, Tyler helped Mr. Jenson inside, visited briefly with Mrs. Jenson, and left. Hailing a cab, he headed to his townhouse.

The next day at the office was very strange. Funeral arrangements had already been made. The funeral would be held on

Thursday at eleven o'clock at a Methodist church in a quiet suburb, with interment in the cemetery behind the church.

Tyler rose early that day and met Brenda for breakfast before dressing for the funeral. He would be a pallbearer. After the brief, sad funeral, he returned to the office to clean up some paperwork that had not been examined since his return from Wyoming. The office was quiet, as the switchboard had been turned off for the day. Tyler was able to wade through the unfinished paperwork and head back to his townhouse around four o'clock.

Slipping out of his suit, Tyler donned a fleece-lined sweat suit and poured a little bourbon over some ice. He settled down in his recliner and opened *Wyoming in Detail*.

The book began with a brief history of the state. Tyler learned that Wyoming had been admitted to the Union on 10 July 1890, and was the forty-fourth state to be admitted. The population at that time was 60,705. Prior to that, it was a territory for twenty-two years. The journey to statehood met with minimal opposition in Congress, though one congressman didn't like the fact that the territorial legislature had granted equal rights to women, including, of all things, the right to vote. Like Arkansas, Florida, and later Hawaii, Wyoming held a constitutional convention without congressional approval, but didn't elect senators or representatives until it had been admitted. Wyoming was a state rich in natural resources. Besides its beautiful mountains and endless sagebrush-covered prairies, it had an abundance of coal and iron ore. In later years, huge oil deposits were discovered. Wild horses and antelope roamed the prairies in massive herds. The mountains were full of elk, deer, and moose. Food was plentiful for the early settlers.

Tyler read on. The southwestern part of the state was where the huge deposits of coal were first discovered. Mining of the coal attracted many workers; among them you could find almost every nationality. Along with the mining came the building of the Union Pacific Railroad. The president of the United States committed to giving the railroad every other section of land for ten miles on either side as an incentive to build. The railroad was badly needed, as there was no way to move the coal from the small Wyoming towns to the parts of the United States that would use it.

The small towns back then were rough and tough. Gambling, prostitution, drinking, and fighting were common pastimes. The miners were well paid for their ventures into the shallow mine shafts, which were infested with rats. The presence of hydrogen sulfide gas made the work even more dangerous. The workers were a tough breed with little culture. Gunfights, fistfights, and brawls were all-too-common events in most of the young mining towns.

Cheyenne was selected to be the capital of the new state, chosen in part because of its location in the extreme southeastern corner, in close proximity to Denver, the capital of Colorado. Cheyenne was also the only town large enough to be named the capital city. The population of modern Wyoming, according to the book, was still under five hundred thousand people, with only one city in the entire state having a population of over fifty thousand.

The book covered the history of the magnificent state in depth. Tyler really enjoyed the reading. It increased his interest in Wyoming to an even higher rate. He wanted to learn more about the state, and he planned to do just that.

Early the next morning Tyler went to the office. The painting he had purchased had arrived, and he proudly placed it on the wall behind his desk. Here, the picture could be viewed by any visitors to his office. It would give him a chance to tell of his new love for the area where he had purchased the painting.

A few evenings later, Tyler started the second book, *Wilderness at Its Best*. It was focused a little more on wildlife and the abundant natural beauty of the state. Tyler pictured himself living in the wilderness and surviving on the land, formulating a dream of becoming a modern mountaineer. He spent hours thinking about how he would handle life and the challenges of living in the wilderness. Tyler convinced himself that he could do it, though it was something he had never seriously considered before. He visualized himself living in a log cabin far from other people, eating fresh fish from the clear icy streams, and surviving on what he could forage from the surrounding environment. Tyler considered potential problems, then solved each of them in his mind. He decided that something like this must be much easier to think about than it was to do, or everyone would be doing it.

Tyler shared his thoughts about Wyoming with Brenda, whose face beamed with delight. Brenda found herself thinking about it more and more. What was the attraction to this place? It was unbearably cold in winter, and one would be hard pressed to find anything social to do, other than traveling to a distant metropolitan area once or twice a year for a culture fix. One would have to love the outdoors, and want to be in it twenty-four hours a day, year-round, to survive such a lonely existence. Is that what Tyler wanted? Is that what Brenda wanted? The thinking and talking continued, dominating both of their minds. They only found relief from their obsession when they were occupied with their work.

Chapter Eight

Spring passed, and the summer was a sizzler. Temperatures reached nearly a hundred degrees for several consecutive days. The investment business had been good, but the loss of one of the Jenson brothers had added more responsibility to Tyler's workload. Tyler had adjusted well, but stress had taken its toll. Tyler found himself getting short with clients and had become more difficult to work with. His normal workday now ran from seven o'clock in the morning to six o'clock in the evening. Many times, he found himself leaving the office after eight o'clock. Tyler began drinking more and more. Every evening he went back to his townhouse feeling sorry for himself, then drank until he went to bed. His relationship with Brenda was virtually nonexistent. He would see her sometimes on the weekends and sleep most of the rest of the time. He was tired. He would go to work with a headache and look at the day through bloodshot, squinting eyes. He had lost weight, and exercise was no longer a priority. Tyler realized he was working and drinking too much. He needed some time off to regroup his mind and prioritize his life. Tyler decided to take a badly needed vacation. He flipped the calendar over and scanned the month of August. He selected the second and third weeks of August and drew a line through them with a pencil. He would take two weeks of vacation then, and save his last week for the autumn.

When he shared his plan with Mr. Jenson, the older man checked his calendar and nodded affirmatively. "That'll be fine, Tyler," he said. "Where you going to go?"

Tyler looked away and responded, "Oh, I'll probably head out west somewhere—maybe to Wyoming. I enjoyed my last visit there. I want to see if it's as great as I remember."

The old man leaned back in his chair and said, "Wyoming? Why the hell would anyone want to go to that Godforsaken place?

I was there twenty years ago, and all I saw that intrigued me was that geyser—'Old Faithful,' I think it's called. You know, that geyser that blows hot water up in the air every few minutes or so. It's kind of weird. But then, not everyone enjoys the Caribbean, which is where I like to go for relaxation. To each his own, I guess. Make sure you bring me up to date on what's going on before you leave. I'll have to baby-sit all those semi-executives while you're gone, and I'll need all the help I can get."

"No problem," Tyler responded. "I'll make sure you have the scoop well in advance of my leaving. I'll check in a couple of times to make certain things are going well while I'm gone. You'll get along fine, I'm sure."

Tyler couldn't wait to tell Brenda about his plans. She had only three weeks to get her arrangements made. She'd better not cop out on me, Tyler thought. It just wouldn't be the same out there without her. After all, she introduced me to the place.

Brenda was jubilant when Tyler gave her the news. She couldn't wait to spend time with him. She was hoping they could renew their relationship. Perhaps they could elevate their feelings for one another to a higher level. Brenda no longer knew where she stood with Tyler. He had changed. He wouldn't joke and frolic with her as he had in the beginning, and he was drinking entirely too much to suit her. Perhaps getting away would help that. Brenda was well aware of Tyler's pressures at work, and of the long, tedious hours he was spending on the job. Brenda blamed Tyler's job for how rarely he spent time with her. It had to be the job; she hadn't done anything to drive him away. Brenda was not a possessive person—in fact, quite the contrary. She was a free spirit who liked no fences. She had handled Tyler's absence and lack of attention remarkably well, but she shuddered at the thought of losing his friendship. Tyler had firmly planted his roots in her heart. She loved him, had since their second date, and likely would forever.

Tyler was happy that the time he had selected for his vacation was acceptable to Brenda. He really wanted her along. Being lonely was not what he needed. Alone, he would undoubtedly spend his vacation drinking to excess, rather than enjoying his time away from work.

Before their vacation, Tyler shopped for more clothes and other items for backpacking expeditions. He wanted more experience in surviving in the wilderness. Tyler had read all the available books on the subject that he could find at the local outfitter's store. He made a list of essential items, and found most of what he needed locally. The rest he ordered from catalogs. Tyler was well equipped for their vacation when the time finally arrived.

Brenda had also prepared herself well for the trip. Tyler had briefed her on what she would need, based on the information in the books he had read. Brenda was looking forward to camping. She had never camped before, and the thought of it excited her. Living out of a backpack, carrying your bed with you, and sleeping under the stars—it all sounded like fun. Best of all, she would be with Tyler. That would make the trip worthwhile. Brenda did have some concern about what they would eat. She had never tried the dehydrated food that Tyler had shown her. The thought of having to eat it for several days left an element of doubt in her mind. What about showers? she wondered. I've never gone more than a day or so without one. I hope Tyler will be understanding.

The time was close and Tyler had nearly finished packing. He had one large duffel bag, which was crammed to the limit. Brenda was having a hard time trying to get all the stuff that she had purchased for the trip into one bag, as well. She wouldn't be taking any dressy clothes on this trip. The previous trip had proven that none were needed. Finally, everything was in the duffel and the zipper was forced closed. Then came the inevitable thought—What have I forgotten? Brenda checked her list over and over for items that she had possibly forgotten to include. She finally gave up, realizing it was impossible to remember everything. Brenda felt she was ready at last. Their flight left at 6:43 the next morning. She retired early and rolled around in the bed for several hours before she fell asleep.

Brenda and Tyler had an uneventful airplane trip and arrived safely in Wyoming. They stayed at the same Western hotel and rented the same little room. They had scarcely settled in the room when Tyler picked up the phone to contact the Rocking R Ranch, a guide and outfitter that he had read about in one of the outdoor magazines. He made arrangements to rent three horses for seven days—two well-broken saddle horses and one packhorse. They could ride into the mountains, set up a small camp, and do most of their exploring on foot. The horses would be available for longer journeys when needed.

Tyler and Brenda left the hotel and walked to a small outdoor shop to purchase some topographical maps, which would provide them with the information they needed to select an area to explore. Tyler spent the extra two dollars to purchase waterproof maps. They also purchased a small two-man tent that rolled up into a small pouch. Next, they walked a short distance to a grocery store to purchase a few perishable items they would need. "I think that's it," Tyler said as they walked back to the hotel. They were ready to tackle the wild, and pursue a new adventure that had been on their minds since they left Wyoming some time ago.

Chapter Nine

The first day of their adventure started with a ride up to Rocking R Ranch in a rented jeep. They arrived at mid-morning and found Lee Thomas, the proprietor, busy currycombing a white stocking-footed sorrel mare in the corral.

Lee was a slim man with a face that reflected years of exposure to the weather—wrinkled and hard, like the faces of the cowboys you see in pictures. He was attired in the traditional Western outfit—Levi's and a plaid shirt. His boots looked for all the world like they were at least ten years old, and had probably been resoled at least three times. The buckle on his belt was engraved with a scene of a cowboy riding a saddled bronco. Across the bottom was the inscription "Champion 1974." The belt was a little long, and the tail hung down the front of his Levi's. Lee's bushy, dark mustache was graying in spots; Tyler guessed his age to be somewhere in the mid-forties. Lee wore a black cowboy hat, which appeared as though it had been the sole survivor of a buffalo stampede.

Tyler parked the jeep and slid through the split-rail fence. He approached Lee in a relaxed, casual fashion. "Are you Lee?" Tyler asked.

"Yes, sir. Welcome to the Rocking R," Lee responded, his hand extended for a cordial handshake. "Nice to see you. You must be—Tyler, is it?"

Tyler grinned, shook Lee's hand, and said, "Nice day, huh! Came to get the lowdown on horse wrangling from the expert."

"Naw, I'm not an expert, I've just got a lot of experience," Lee commented. He never stopped combing the mare. Perhaps he was a little apprehensive about trusting his horses to a Chicago tenderfoot. "You leaving tomorrow?" he asked.

"That's our plan," Tyler said, and motioned to Brenda to come meet Lee.

Brenda climbed from the jeep and slipped through the fence. "Hi, I'm Brenda," she said as she approached.

"Pleased to make your acquaintance, ma'am," Lee said.

Brenda turned and examined the sorrel mare. "This is a beautiful horse. May I pet him?"

"Sure," Lee said. "It's a she, and she's one of my better mares. She loves attention, especially from pretty ladies." Lee grinned and patted the mare on the neck. It was clear that Lee also had some admiration for pretty ladies. "We've got a lot of work to do, if you're leaving tomorrow," Lee said. "Better get started. It takes a while to teach the essentials of horsing."

The rest of the morning and afternoon was spent with Lee, as he carefully explained how to care for horses in the mountains. The training covered feeding, when to water, and hobbling, all of which was new to Tyler and Brenda.

"Hobbling is the most important thing you have to remember," Lee said. "If you hobble the horses properly, they can water and feed themselves."

Hobbling, he explained, involved attaching a thick leather belt-like device with a buckle on each end to each of the horse's front feet, just above the bottom knuckle on the leg, above the hoof. When the hobble is installed it leaves about eighteen inches of slack, allowing the horse to take only small steps. Normally, another leather strap, about thirty-six inches long, is snapped to the horse's halter. The other end of the strap is attached to the leather hobble between the horse's front feet. This keeps the animal's head down and makes movement very difficult, prohibiting it from moving too fast or too far. The horses would likely learn to move around more easily by rearing up and moving both feet forward in a kind of hopping manner. A trail-smart horse could move as much as a mile in a six to eight hour period, in spite of the hobble. Smarter horses had to be controlled by shortening the length of the hobble strap and the halter strap so that the horse's head is forced down even further, still allowing the animal to graze and drink. Pretty clever invention, Tyler thought.

Next, they were taught bridling and saddling, and had a brief riding lesson from Lee to make certain they were capable of handling the mounts he had selected for them. The novice riders quickly learned to handle the horses and enjoyed the experience immensely. Lee, on the other hand, was still a little apprehensive about trusting his new acquaintances and their newfound talents with his horses.

It was late in the day when Brenda and Tyler thanked Lee for his patience. They advised him of their plans to depart the ranch at mid-morning the next day, and headed back to the hotel.

Lee unsaddled the mounts and left the corral. He walked over and slid behind the wheel of his well-used, four-wheel-drive pickup truck. He had a few hours left before sundown to check the north fences on the sprawling, three-thousand acre ranch and to find where his cattle were getting out. He was getting tired of riding up to the Box W Ranch to retrieve the animals that had gotten through the fence, mixing with the cattle there. It would take him about three or four hours a day, twice a week, to get his cattle separated and driven home.

The Box W Ranch bordered Lee's ranch on the north side, and extended about three miles to the east. Lee's place was adjacent to land belonging to the Bureau of Land Management—the BLM—on its east side. The Box W Ranch and the Rocking R were the only deeded ranches in the foothills, which were bordered on all sides by BLM land. Excluding them, the closest deeded land was nearly six miles away, back toward the Snake River. Both ranch owners were fortunate to be blessed with forefathers who had the insight to homestead this beautiful land. Lee got along well with the Waltons, the owners of the Box W, which may be considered unusual. Ranchers often found one reason or another not to get along. Lee had heard rumors that the Waltons might be interested in selling, but there was no way he could afford to buy them out. He struggled to survive on his mortgage-free place. The best Lee could hope for was to get lucky enough to have good neighbors, should the Waltons decide to sell. It'll probably be one of those money people from California, Lee thought. Crazy-dude Californians are buying up all the land in the whole damned valley.

Many of the beautiful ranches near Jackson Hole had been purchased by large corporations, and were turned into dude ranches that all the friends and business acquaintances of the higher-ups were invited to visit. They were a bother for the natives, who resisted their exorbitant offers for land purchases. Lee had received some attractive offers, but he was not interested in selling. He enjoyed raising his Hereford cattle, and loved the freedom he felt when he mounted his horse and rode across his ranch. Lee was a true, dyed-in-the-wool rancher—always had been, and likely would be until the day he died.

Chapter Ten

Tyler and Brenda bounced out of bed early the next morning and secured their bags. They were ready for the trip. They went downstairs and ordered the cowboy breakfast from the handwritten menu in the coffee shop—three eggs prepared the way you like them, a slice of country-cured ham, hash browns, sourdough toast, orange juice, and coffee. Brenda stuffed herself, knowing this would be the last decent meal she would eat for a few days. Tyler ate everything on his plate and finished the last piece of Brenda's toast, which was thickly covered with strawberry preserves.

"Ready to hit the trail, buckaroo?" Tyler asked as he reached over and tenderly pinched Brenda on the cheek.

"I'm ready, cowboy," she said, grinning and content from the much-too-large breakfast. Returning to the room, Brenda and Tyler carefully placed their Western hats on their heads and headed to the jeep with their duffels.

Tyler drove the jeep to the Rocking R in silence. His apprehension was beginning to show. The weather was comfortably warm, with a cool breeze that sifted the tall grass in the meadows.

"Perfect day," Tyler said as he fumbled with the radio, hoping to find a long-range weather forecast before departing civilization. He settled for a Merle Haggard tune entitled "Swinging Doors." Merle sang, "I got swinging doors, a jukebox, and a barstool; my new home bears a flashing neon sign. You can find me here anytime you want to; I'm always here at home at closing time." The music fit the mood of the day perfectly.

The couple arrived at the ranch just as Lee was walking to the barn from the ranch house. He placed a large pinch of chewing tobacco under his bottom lip, a customary habit of many cowboys. Tyler pulled the jeep up close to the barn, where it would be out of the way, and shut off the engine, then climbed out and proceeded to unload their gear. Lee came over, made small talk, and grabbed a duffel. The gear was carried over to the barn door, where it could be loaded onto the packhorse.

"We'll need to saddle the riding horses and put the saddle on the packhorse," Lee said as he opened the barn door and placed a bridle on one of the riding horses. He led the same docile gray mare that Tyler had ridden during his training session outside and tied the reins to the top rail of the corral. Then, he brought over two saddles and two saddle blankets, which he dropped carelessly on the ground. "Go ahead and saddle this one. I'll get the other riding horse," he said.

Tyler, remembering his lesson, stood on the proper side of the mare and placed the saddle blanket on its back. Then, he carefully aligned the saddle blanket, as Lee had taught him. He hooked the stirrup onto the saddle horn and placed the saddle on the horse's back, in the middle of the blanket. He then flipped the stirrup from the saddle horn and let it fall down the side of the mare, to its proper place. He reached under the animal and grabbed the cinch strap, and threaded it through the large ring on the saddle. He cinched it tight and tied it off perfectly just as Lee arrived with the sorrel gilding that Brenda would ride.

Tyler proceeded to saddle the sorrel just as he had the bay mare, and Lee went to the barn. He returned leading the packhorse, with a long hemp rope attached to its halter. The packhorse was a short, rather stocky black mare with two white-stocking feet in front and a large white blaze on her forehead. The mare's packsaddle was constructed on a leather base and consisted of two pieces of wood that crossed at the front of the saddle to form an upright X. The rear of the saddle had the same wooden configuration. Two large canvas panniers were affixed to each side of the horse, held in place by two loops, which hooked over the wooden supports.

Tyler placed the duffels in the panniers, then filled the spaces around the duffels with other gear. The backpacks were tied to the top of the packsaddle. Tyler also tied their jackets to the saddle with two long pieces of twang leather. The jackets could easily be reached if needed during a sudden mountain shower. Tyler hung the canvas water bag on his saddle horn, and Brenda wrapped the strap of a small leather utility bag containing their lunch around her saddle horn.

Lee went over the map with Tyler and selected a spot close to a spring-fed lake, at about nine thousand feet, where he suggested the main camp should be set. Lee also pointed out areas of the map containing dangerous terrain as places Brenda and Lee should avoid. Lee explained to Tyler that if they weren't back on Tuesday he would come looking for them. God forbid, Brenda thought.

The spot Lee had selected for the camp was nearly nine miles away. Lee cautioned the riders to take it slow and easy and to stop occasionally to rest and water the horses.

The riders climbed up on the horses, said good-bye to Lee, and headed off into the mountains. Tyler led the packhorse and followed Brenda, who rode in front. They headed down the path, which followed the fence line separating the Box W Ranch from the Rocking R. The scenery was beautiful. The snowcapped mountains reached toward the heavens, with beautiful lodgepole pines protruding above the pockets of colorful aspens that covered the foothills. It was gorgeous, just as they had expected it to be. Brenda, inspired, felt a little brave and a whole lot scared.

It was approaching lunch time when Tyler pulled his horse to a stop. He dismounted and tied the horses to a limb of a fallen aspen, then raised up on his toes to stretch his legs, which were already feeling the stress of the ride. Brenda and Tyler each ate a banana and munched down a chocolate bar, then lay down on the thick green grass and soaked up the warm rays of the summer sun.

It was a bit of an empty feeling to know they were on their own, totally responsible for the horses and their own well-being, but so far, things were going well. The horses had traveled slowly and steadily, as though they knew exactly where they were headed with their riders. Brenda hoped the horses knew where they were headed, since she had no earthly idea.

After the sparse lunch and a brief rest they mounted the horses and proceeded onward and upward, into the mountains. Tyler was plotting their course on the map and seemed to know what he was doing.

It was late afternoon when they arrived at the lake where they would set up their camp. Tyler examined the area and selected a grassy spot in a small clearing close to the lake. Behind the clearing were a few trees that bordering a small meadow. There was evidence that the campsite had been used before. Completing the task of unloading the packhorse, Tyler set up the small tent where they would sleep. After a short trip to the lake to give the horses a drink, they hobbled the animals and released them for evening grazing. The horses slowly worked their way to the meadow and lay down to rest. They would graze later.

The evening meal consisted of dehydrated beef stew and crackers. It tasted good, much better than Brenda had expected. Either the food was really good, or she was very hungry. Tired, sore, and with full stomachs, the wilderness travelers unrolled their sleeping bags next to the small fire that Tyler had built and relaxed. Darkness had fallen, and Tyler gazed up at the stars. Never had they seemed so radiant and bright. The tired campers soon fell asleep under the beautiful starlit sky.

The next morning, the blinding sun woke them. Tyler crawled from his sleeping bag and built a small fire to brew some coffee. Brenda waited until the coffee was ready before crawling from her sleeping bag, still fully attired.

"You slept with your clothes on?" Tyler asked.

"Yes, I did. I was afraid I would get cold," Brenda responded.

"You should never get in a sleeping bag with your clothes on," Tyler said. "Your clothes get damp during the day, and sleeping in them will make you cold. I read that in a wilderness book before we left."

"Not me," Brenda responded. "You won't catch me out here running around in the wilderness with no clothes on."

"You could crawl in my bag with me, if you're scared," Tyler said.

"Then I would wear my clothes for sure," Brenda said as she smiled and winked.

Brenda was so beautiful, Tyler thought. He was proud of her and how well she was adapting to the adventure. She looked great out in the woods, even with uncombed hair and freshly out of a sleeping bag—a claim few women or men can make.

Chapter Eleven

The day went well. There were no catastrophes of any conse-quence, except a minor incident that occurred when Tyler was attempting to put the hobbles on the horses after returning from a ride. Attempting to tighten one end of the strap, Tyler had slipped and fallen backward. This frightened the mare, which bolted free, breaking the reins that secured the animal to a tree. Tyler quickly jumped up and chased the animal. Brenda laughed at the sight of him chasing the playful creature. After several minutes of attempt-ing to catch up with the mare, the horse trotted down to the lake and began drinking. Brenda walked over and grabbed the reins that hung from the bridle. Dumbass horse, Tyler thought as he led the creature back to the grazing area. Tyler had sprained his wrist when he fell, but it was not too serious.

The campers slept in the tent that night, since it was starting to cloud up and threatening to rain. Lightning was dancing on the hori-zon, and thunder could be heard echoing in the distance.

On the morning of the third day, the sun was shining under a cloudless blue sky. The rain hadn't arrived, but a cool breeze greeted them as they rose and crawled out of the small tent. Tyler headed to a little clump of mountain birch trees to relieve his aching blad-der. Then it was Brenda's turn. Tyler put a pot of coffee on the kin-dled fire and spread the map out on the grass. He spotted a small lake above where they were camped, and decided it would be a nice hike to follow the meandering creek up the mountain to the lake; it was called "Arrowhead Lake," apparently after its triangular shape. The trip would be about a mile and a half, if Tyler was reading the map correctly. The climb appeared to be steep to Tyler, based on the countless lines on the map between their campsite and the upper lake. According to the map legend, each line represented ten feet of elevation, and there were probably twenty between the lake and where they were camped.

After a snack of rye crackers and Swiss cheese, Brenda and Tyler finished the last of the coffee and donned their backpacks to begin the journey. They wouldn't use the horses today.

The map was accurate, and the climb proved to be tedious and treacherous. The air was thin, and breathing came hard with the added weight of their backpacks. Footing was terrible, and they were forced to rest often. When they stopped they marveled at the beautiful wildflowers that swayed in the breeze. The colors were magnificent. The stream was full of little wild brook trout that darted from rock to rock, attempting to hide when the hikers cast shadows on the water.

It took the couple nearly two hours to hike to the upper lake. The lake was beautiful, about half the size of the one they had camped by. Its shoreline was covered with huge granite boulders, sitting majestically as if to hold the water in place. Two beavers were lazily swimming around the lake's upper end, dragging branches and twigs to the large mound they were erecting for their home. The lake was fed by several small streams, which worked their way down across a swampy aspen grove on its far end. The water was fresh and clear. Brenda and Tyler removed their hiking boots and hung their feet in the cool water, sitting on a large rock. It felt great on their tired, hot feet.

Afterward, the couple put their boots on, stowed their backpacks by a boulder, and left to explore the upper end of the lake. They found the walking difficult. The ground was water-soaked, and their feet were swallowed by the black, gooey mud. Often, they would sink in above their hiking boots before firm footing could be found. Walking got worse the further they attempted to venture. Just as Tyler had made up his mind to turn back, a startled animal bolted and jumped from a thick growth of heavy bushes twenty feet to their left. The animal stopped and faced them in silence. It was a moose calf. It was all legs, and it swayed back and forth, struggling to stay on top of them. Brenda was excited. "Oh, Tyler, it's so cute. What is it? It's a baby—is it lost?"

"Be careful, Brenda, it's a moose," Tyler responded.

Suddenly, the huge mother moose came crashing through the brush, its ears tilted forward and its head held high, snorting as if to let the intruders know she meant business. She stopped just short of her calf, which quickly retreated to her side. The mother moose sniffed the little animal to make certain it was all right, then jumped directly at the two intruders with her head down, snorting loudly.

Is she going to charge? Tyler wondered. Cautiously, he reached for Brenda and slowly moved her behind him. Brenda was scared to death. The determined moose just stood there, ten feet away, not giving an inch. Tyler was afraid to move. He was petrified. As quietly as he could, he turned his head and whispered instructions to Brenda to slowly retreat. She carefully backed away from Tyler, one cautious step at a time. It was difficult, as she had to struggle to pull her feet from the stubborn mud. The moose never moved. The huge animal stared Tyler directly in the eye, daring him to advance and towering over the intruder. She was either very brave or bluffed better than Tyler had ever seen before.

After what seemed like an eternity, Tyler slowly turned his head to see how far Brenda had gone. She had made it to the edge of the swamp and was running frantically toward a large pine tree to seek safety up its trunk.

Judgment time had arrived for Tyler. He glanced around the area and spotted a piece of timber lying near his feet. Slowly, he bent his knees and lowered his arms to grasp his chosen weapon. The moose still didn't move. Tyler grasped the timber and gripped it securely on one end, then slowly returned to an upright position, holding the timber at his side. Suddenly, the moose charged, head down, mouth open, revealing what seemed like a thousand big, ugly teeth. Tyler jumped to the side, raised the timber, and slammed it across the head of his attacker. Unaffected, the moose swung around and charged again. This time, Tyler couldn't move. With his feet firmly planted in the deep mud, he was helpless. The head of the huge moose caught him under the left arm, on the rib cage. Tyler was slung face-down into the mud, with the timber still in his right hand. He was hurt; immediate pain paralyzed his whole left side. As best he could, Tyler rolled over, raised the timber, and poked the relentless animal in the face, hoping to hit an eye or tender spot on the huge animal. The moose tossed its head to the side, knocking the timber from Tyler's hand as if it were a matchstick.

Tyler was now completely defenseless. The animal continued to swing its huge head, making contact with the helpless human with every pass. Tyler placed his hands over his face and prayed to God that the moose would stop inflicting pain on his now limp, suffering body. He realized he was lucky that this was a cow moose and not an antlered bull.

Tyler was close to losing consciousness. He lay motionless, barely breathing in the watery, muddy swamp. The moose ran in a half circle and stopped about fifteen feet away, facing her enemy. She began nervously tossing her head about, searching for her calf, who had moved into the brush. The calf was out of sight, and the cow raised her head high and trotted after it. Tyler could hear the two of them crashing through the brush for several minutes as they fled the scene of the confrontation.

When Brenda felt it was safe, she rushed to check on Tyler, who she felt certain was dead. When she arrived at his side, he was unconscious. What could she do? She placed her fingers on his neck, frantically searching for a pulse. He was still alive. She must get him out of the swamp.

Brenda began slapping Tyler lightly on the cheeks to wake him, increasing the intensity of the blows with each effort. Finally, Tyler opened his eyes and looked at her as if in a drunken stupor.

"The moose is gone. Lie still," Brenda instructed. "Can you move your legs?"

Tyler, grimacing with pain, managed to mumble, "I think so." After a few moments, he slowly moved each leg to assess the damage. They weren't broken—badly bruised and sprained, but not broken. After several minutes, with great pain and effort and Brenda's help, Tyler was able to roll over onto his chest and pull his knees up under his body. He dragged himself from the swamp, pushing his body upright with his arms. He rested on all fours and continued to cautiously check his body for damage. Both arms were fine, but he was sure he had broken ribs on his left side. Breathing was labored and dreadfully painful.

With Brenda's help, Tyler attempted to stand. He fell back to his knees and grabbed his side. "I can't do it, I can't do it. The pain—it's my chest!"

Brenda was sobbing now. "Tyler, you have to! Please try again—please." Brenda wiped the tears wildly from her cheeks and reached for his right arm, desperately trying to help him stand. After several attempts, Tyler finally raised his aching body to an upright position.

Brenda was wild with fright and was visibly shaking. Tyler placed his right hand on her shoulder for support and wiped the mud from his face and eyes. "Settle down, Brenda, I'll make it now.

Just give me a minute to clear my head." He stood for a moment before trying to take a step. There was a loud sucking sound as the mud unwillingly surrendered his captured foot. Slowly, painfully, Tyler moved each foot, taking short, careful steps for what seemed like an eternity. It took several minutes for them to reach dry, firm ground. Walking was a little less painful and much faster now that they were out of the mud. Tyler made it to a large granite boulder and sat down on the rock to rest. He assessed the damage to his mangled body.

"Brenda, would you go get that timber I used to fight off the moose? It'll make a good crutch."

Brenda waded into the swamp and recovered the timber. She returned and handed it to Tyler, who looked it over in great detail. He then placed it on the ground, testing its strength. With the help of the timber and Brenda, he stood and slowly headed for the area where they had stowed their backpacks. Carefully, painfully, Tyler hobbled his way through the boulders and rocks. The short trip seemed like miles.

Brenda took a large paper towel from her backpack and dipped it in the cool water of the lake, then gently wiped Tyler's face, trying to clean and refresh him as much as possible. His right eye was starting to swell, and he had a small, bruised cut on his chin, the only damage Brenda could see. Of course, hurt pride can't be seen with the naked eye.

After a lengthy rest they proceeded back to the base camp. Travel was slow, and they were forced to stop regularly so Tyler could rest. Brenda frequently wiped Tyler's face with the towel, which she kept damp with cool water from the creek. Though the trip was all downhill, it was taking much more time than the trip uphill had. At last, they made it down to the level ground around the lake, and walking became much easier. They arrived at the campsite just as the sun was sinking below the horizon.

Tyler was relieved to be back at their camp, and was especially happy to be able to lie down. He would feel better after some badly needed rest. Brenda fumbled through her backpack and found a bottle of aspirin. She gave three tablets to Tyler. He swallowed hard, forcing them into his stomach, and chased them with a glass of water from the water bag. Laying his head down, he closed his eyes and dozed. Brenda lit a camp candle and softly rubbed his forehead as he rested. When Brenda was sure he was sound asleep, she blew out the candle and crawled into her sleeping bag, after a short prayer. She was happy to see this day come to an end.

Chapter Twelve

Morning came quickly. Brenda crawled from her sleeping bag and made some coffee as Tyler slept. It was nearly an hour later when Tyler stirred. Cautiously, he crawled from his sleeping bag and raised himself upright. He was slumped slightly from the pain in his rib cage, but he felt somewhat better.

Tyler shuffled over to Brenda, who had poured him a cup of hot, steaming coffee. He sipped it, carefully sitting down on a nearby boulder. His eye was black and blue and badly swollen, and judging from the pain, the attacking moose had either broken or cracked some ribs.

"Do we have something we could wrap around my chest for support?" he asked.

Brenda walked over to his duffel bag and returned with a T-shirt. "I'll make a support from this," she said, holding the shirt up for Tyler to see. With a quick pull, she ripped it along the seam underneath the sleeve. She carefully wrapped the fabric around Tyler's rib cage, tying it as tightly as she dared. Though crude, it provided some support, which helped.

"Would you like to load up and head back?" Brenda asked.

"I'll be fine, if you're willing to stay," Tyler responded.

"Don't you think you should see a doctor?"

"No, I'll just take it easy, and see how I feel tomorrow."

The rest of the daylight hours were spent lying around camp and discussing the events of the previous day. Brenda and Tyler felt extremely lucky to be alive. They reconstructed the incident several times in their conversation. It was a restful day, spent relaxing and visiting. They retired early.

The next morning, Tyler felt a little better. He found he could move about a bit more freely. After a morning stroll to check on the horses, he and Brenda took a short hike to the other side of the lake.

They proceeded with caution, making sure not to startle any more wildlife. They had learned their lesson.

They rested again that afternoon. Tyler removed a pencil and pad from his duffel and attempted to sketch a picture of the lovely mountains. Though he had never done anything like this before, he managed to complete a sketch that wasn't too bad. The drawing closely resembled the scene, with its beautiful mountain peaks and trees.

Brenda was surprised at the remarkable beauty that Tyler was able to capture in his picture. She smiled and proudly held the finished product up in the air. "I'll keep it forever, Tyler. I love it." She propped the pad on a small limb in a tree nearby and backed away to admire it. Tyler was so talented. He could do almost anything he set out to do, she thought.

The rest of their camping trip was spent taking short hikes and nature walks. Tyler continued to sketch, a newly discovered talent that provided a lot of satisfaction. It was amazing how he seemed to have a natural ability to capture the scenery with nothing but a number-three pencil and a sketch pad.

The day had arrived and it was time to head back. Though still sore and feeling a lot of pain, Tyler was able to retrieve the horses and saddle them for their return to the ranch. They filled the panniers on the packhorses, and Tyler made sure to place the timber used to stave off the moose among their belongings. After a brief search of the area to make certain it was tidy, the two wilderness adventurers mounted their horses and began the trip back to the Rocking R.

The journey was slow and uneventful. Tyler was not too comfortable riding the horse, as his ribs ached with every step the lumbering animal took. They felt sad as they left the beautiful countryside, but Tyler was happy when he saw Lee's barn finally come into view.

It was early evening by the time they had returned the horses and told Lee their stories. Lee listened in amazement.

"Nothing meaner than a moose cow with a young calf," he told them. "They can really get surly."

The three of them visited for over an hour, discussing every little event of their adventuresome stay in the mountains.

Brenda and Tyler thanked Lee for his hospitality, loaded their gear in the jeep, and headed to town. They arrived back at the hotel at dusk and wasted no time getting to their room. The thought of a warm shower had been on their minds for the last few days. The hot water felt great, as they expected it would. The soft bed was wonderful too, and they fell asleep in each other's arms, dreaming of the beautiful mountains they had left, enjoying the feel of their warm, naked bodies. It was a little bit of heaven.

Brenda woke early the next morning and found Tyler studying the map and making notes on a scratch pad. He informed Brenda of his plan to do a little exploring in the jeep that day. But first they took a trip to the doctor's office, which confirmed Tyler's suspicion. He had cracked two ribs, and though it was painful, he would be fine. The doctor advised him to take it easy and not do any heavy lifting. He gave Tyler a wraparound elastic brace, which was a little more comfortable than the one Brenda had made for him.

Relieved, they left the doctor's office, got in the jeep, and headed north on the course that Tyler had penciled in on the map. He had spotted another road on the map that appeared to fork off from the one that led to the Rocking R, about six miles beyond the turnoff to Lee's ranch. They found the road, which was actually a trail, and drove the jeep along it. It seemed to head nowhere, going in the same general direction as they had headed the previous week, but veering a little more to the north.

Travel was slow. The trail was full of rocks and boulders, which demanded a lot of maneuvering. They stopped about an hour later, since a huge granite boulder blocked any further travel in the jeep. Brenda and Tyler proceeded on foot from there.

"What are we looking for, Tyler?" Brenda wanted to know.

"Nothing, Brenda. Just looking," he responded.

However, Brenda knew he was too intense to be "just looking." They soon topped a small hill that overlooked a large, grassy meadow. Straining his eyes and squinting, Tyler could see a sizable lake, which appeared to be three or four miles away.

"There it is," Tyler said, pointing to his map, which he had spread out on a flat rock. "I knew we could find it! Eagle Lake— that's it. Elevation is 7700 feet. The lake has about four miles of shoreline, and it's supposed to be 150 feet deep. It's a glacier lake," Tyler said excitedly. "The water is so pure that it can be drunk without treatment. It's full of trout, and the closest road is the one we just came up. It tells all about it here on the back of the map, see?"

Tyler and Brenda were suddenly surprised by a horse and rider coming down the hill on their left. The rider spotted them and reined his mount in their direction. Approaching, the cowboy raised his hand, Indian-style, as if to signal that he was a friend. Lonely, friendly, and talkative, the rider acted as if he hadn't seen a human for days.

The rider turned out to be Mr. Walton, the owner of the ranch adjoining the Rocking R Ranch. Mr. Walton was a true cowboy, well past middle age. He explained to Brenda and Tyler that he was up on BLM land looking for stray cattle. He asked if they had seen any cattle bearing the Box W brand, which was his family's longtime registered brand. They visited for quite some time with Mr. Walton, who seemed like a nice, respectable country gentleman. He expounded on his ancestry and how proud he was to be a Wyoming cowboy.

Tyler was full of questions about the lake, the surrounding mountains, and the area in general. Mr. Walton answered his questions, and seemed to be quite knowledgeable about the area. He explained that he had lived here since he was a child. Discovering that Brenda and Tyler were from Chicago, he mentioned that he had a cousin there. "Someday I plan to come look him up," he said.

As Mr. Walton was about to leave, Tyler dug a business card out of his wallet and handed it to him. He insisted that it would be nice to have Mr. Walton call if he ever came to Chicago. This made Mr. Walton chuckle, and he vowed to contact Tyler if he ever made it to "the big city." After more small talk, Mr. Walton climbed up on his mount and headed back in the direction from which he had come.

"Interesting gentleman," Tyler commented.

Brenda and Tyler stood for several more minutes, holding hands and gazing into the distance as if in a trance. The loved each other, and they loved this country.

During the trip back to the jeep, Tyler found himself walking much more easily, with less pain. Having the doctor ascertain that he had no serious injuries had helped Tyler as much as anything else. For some reason, the human mind rests easier when told by a professional that everything is fine. The mind is funny sometimes.

The vacation had come to an end. The duffel bags were packed, and the trip back to Chicago and its "city life" would soon be reality. The next morning, Brenda and Tyler would leave this beautiful country.

Tyler and Brenda were remorseful on the trip back to Chicago. They had now experienced life in the wilderness, and they both wanted more. They had loved every part of it, excluding the moose encounter, of course. Their Chicago friends would never believe the story. Most of their friends had never seen a moose, much less danced with one. Tyler had, and he would never forget it. The piece of timber went back to Chicago with him. It would be the topic of many future conversations. It was a true wilderness souvenir.

Chapter Thirteen

Back in Chicago, things hadn't changed. The market, though a little weak, was holding steady, having peaked on Tuesday of the previous week and dropping a few points toward the week's end. Tyler had learned to check his portfolio immediately upon returning from days away from work. He had aligned it in such a way that it gave him a diverse overview of the market trends in his absence. After a quick look he found that he had managed to pick up a few dollars while he was gone.

Tyler had been in the office most of the morning after the sweat-pit when Mr. Jenson entered.

"Tyler, welcome back. It seems like you've been gone half the summer. Did you enjoy your vacation?"

"It was super. I nearly met my Waterloo, but I escaped with just a few scars."

Tyler told Mr. Jenson every last detail of his trip, carefully describing the moose encounter. Mr. Jenson listened with great curiosity. When he had finished, Mr. Jenson sat in the chair, closely examining the timber. Tyler had brought it to the office to make the story more realistic. Mr. Jenson put the timber back in the corner where it had been propped and returned to the guest chair.

"Tyler, I have been wanting to talk with you about the firm. I have given this considerable thought, and I want to make you a proposition—a business proposition."

Tyler listened with great interest as Mr. Jenson related how he had little interest in the business since the loss of his brother. He praised Tyler, noting how well he had adapted to his added responsibilities and how he was liked by the customers and other staff members. He finished by saying that he wanted to sell the business, and that he would like Tyler to buy it.

This took Tyler completely by surprise. Where would he get the money to make a purchase like that? He didn't know what to say. He told Mr. Jenson how flattered he was to be considered a candidate, but insisted that he would need some time to think about it. This was not in Tyler's plan, and he was not prepared to discuss it in detail. Mr. Jenson understood that it would require some thought, and he left the office, saying they would discuss it later in more detail.

For the rest of the day, Tyler's mind was occupied with questions. Prior to Mr. Jenson's visit, Tyler's thoughts were more along the lines of how to get out of the business, not how to get in deeper. Now he was really confused.

That evening, he told Brenda about the conversation he had with Mr. Jenson. In her apartment, she sat beside him and listened intently, pledging her support if Tyler elected to pursue the acquisition. They spent the entire evening discussing the possibilities. Talking to Brenda gave Tyler a chance to think out loud as questions arose in his busy mind. He talked on and on, discussing the debt he would incur and the time it would require to satisfy the lender, the obvious changes that would have to be made within the organization, the people involved, and lastly, the potentially large sum of money that could be made.

The conversation went on well past midnight. Brenda was a good listener, and encouraged Tyler to not make a hasty decision. She told him she would continue to love him if he elected to give it a try, and would also continue to love him if he didn't. Tyler found it comforting to know that he had Brenda's support.

Finally, at three o'clock in the morning, Tyler kissed Brenda on the cheek and headed back to his townhouse. The air was humid and warm as he walked quickly down the empty street. He arrived home safely and went to bed. He couldn't sleep; his mind was on overload. It was a short night.

Tyler spent the next three weeks visiting with bankers, lawyers, and insurance companies, gathering all the information he could about potential venture. He wanted all the questions answered. After all, this would be a giant step for him, and he had to make every effort he could to ascertain that the decision he made was the right one. Never once did the question of his ability to be successful enter his mind. He knew his capabilities. His decision would be entirely based on the issues of money and finances. He was sure he could manage the people and the business.

To pass the time and help himself think, Tyler had invested in some acrylic paints, brushes and an easel. He would sit and practice his painting while thinking about the acquisition. Brenda visited nearly every day, and marveled at how well he was doing with his art while listening to his comments about his progress on the potential acquisition. Tyler painted pictures extracted from his memories of the beautiful Wyoming scenery. His love for Brenda and Wyoming was slowly taking over his mind. He wanted the two of them much more than he wanted Jenson and Jenson.

As time passed, Tyler realized that he was not interested in tying himself to a business and working in Chicago until he died. He had made up his mind. He would not purchase the firm. He must advise Mr. Jenson of his decision so the older man could pursue finding another buyer. Tyler would tell Mr. Jenson the next morning.

He arrived at work early. The morning was filled with the activities of a normal workday. There were numerous phone calls and lots of paperwork. Around ten o'clock, he walked to Mr. Jenson's office. Mr. Jenson was reading the *Wall Street Journal*, which he neatly folded and placed on his desk as Tyler entered.

"Yes, Tyler. Sit down. What's on your mind?"

Tyler told Mr. Jenson of his decision not to purchase the firm. Mr. Jenson was obviously disappointed. However, being the gentleman that he was, he told Tyler that he understood, and that he hoped Tyler would continue to work for the firm. A long discussion followed, covering the pros and cons of owning the firm. Mr. Jenson mentioned that there was another interested buyer, and he would contact him to see if the interest was casual or sincere. The conversation ended with a congenial handshake. Mr. Jenson told Tyler he would keep him informed of his progress.

Tyler left the office and returned to his desk to call Brenda. He liked Mr. Jenson, and felt badly that he had disappointed him, but he was relieved to have gotten the potential purchase off his mind.

Work continued as usual for the next few weeks. Mr. Jenson was busy in private meetings with potential buyers for the firm. Tyler became more and more convinced that he had made the right decision—to decline Mr. Jenson's offer.

It was in the sweat-pit that Mr. Jenson announced that a deal had been made and the firm had been sold. He briefly went over the intended timing of the sale and discussed the principals involved. It came as no surprise to the staff members. It was common knowledge around the office that Mr. Jenson was actively soliciting prospective buyers for the firm. Mr. Jenson assured his staff that there would be no dramatic changes in personnel for the time being; nonetheless, his assurance did not make everyone feel totally confident. Anything could happen when the new owner took over. The new owners would take over the following Monday, and the contracts would be signed on or about the first of October. Mr. Jenson would be leaving the firm shortly thereafter. It was a struggle for him to make the announcement. After all, the firm had been his lifeblood for over thirty-three years. Leaving would not be easy. He ended his speech by praising the employees and expounding on how he would miss them. He invited everyone to visit him in Florida. He planned to move there before Christmas, if everything went smoothly.

As Mr. Jenson left the room, a few tears worked their way down his saddened, wrinkled face. His entire life had been spent building the investment business with his brother, and developing an irreproachable reputation. This was a tough day for Mr. Jenson.

Chapter Fourteen

The work environment didn't change much under the new owner. Tyler continued to be one of the senior investment officers; however, he was no longer the person in charge of conducting the sweat-pit. The new chief executive officer, Vincent Larson, felt he should conduct this meeting as a way of becoming familiar with the staff. Tyler enjoyed the meetings much more as an attendee, so this was a welcome change.

Mr. Larson, though well-versed in the investment market, depended heavily on Tyler. He had spent some time monitoring Tyler's performance, and quickly recognized that he was a professional and a born leader. Tyler liked Mr. Larson, in part because he knew the man recognized and respected his abilities.

Tyler also continued to do well for himself. His personal portfolio had grown to a point where he could probably retire whenever he desired. He enjoyed his work, and made a nice salary, but somehow he couldn't get Wyoming out of his mind. Was he too young to retire? Would he be happy with no job to report to each day? And what about Brenda? He wanted her to be part of his plans.

Tyler continued to paint, pondering in his mind the possibility of retiring and moving to Wyoming. Hours were spent in contemplation of what he wanted to do with the rest of his life. He read and studied life in the wilderness. He had visions of himself in a log cabin in the mountains, living off the land, enjoying life, painting, and becoming friends with the wildlife—excluding the moose. The one thing that never seemed quite clear to Tyler was how Brenda would fit into this scheme.

After a nice dinner at a quaint French restaurant, halfway through their second bottle of wine, Tyler sprang the idea on Brenda.

"Brenda, how would you like to move to Wyoming?"

Brenda's eyes became wide and her mouth dropped open. "Tyler, have you lost your mind? How could we do that?"

"We just do it," Tyler said. "Just pack up all our stuff and move to Wyoming. We could live on my investment income. Find us a nice little place up in the mountains where I could paint and you could do whatever you want. I'm sure you'd find something to do. I really want to do it, Brenda. I want you to come with me."

Brenda stared into her wineglass, as if hypnotized. A small, sweet smile blossomed on her pretty face, but the rest of her was still, as if cast in stone. Shaking her head slowly, she responded, "I . . . I think I'm in shock, Tyler. This whole idea is a total surprise to me. I don't know what to think."

Tyler reached for her hand and grasped it firmly, saying, "Brenda, let's do it. We would be happy. We both love Wyoming, and we should live there."

Brenda took a deep breath and looked Tyler in the eye for some time before responding. "Tyler, you know I love you—I always will. But this is going to require some serious thinking. My job . . . I can't just walk out. Besides, this whole thing is too sudden for me. I need some time."

"Fine, Brenda," Tyler replied, "take all the time you need. I realize you're dedicated to the company, and that you enjoy your job. But, if you'll go with me, I'm prepared to give up everything and go. We don't have to go in the next few days. We can take as much time as we need to tie up all the loose ends."

They finished up the last of the wine and strolled arm in arm down the street to Brenda's place. Brenda slept very little that night. Had Tyler lost his mind? she wondered. Was he serious? Could he really do it? Could she?

For several days, Brenda explored the idea of moving to Wyoming. She would just about be ready to commit when a sickening feeling of insecurity would overtake her. The thought scared her to death, and she didn't want to talk about it. She acted as though the whole idea didn't exist when Tyler was around. He sensed Brenda's reluctance, and never brought up the subject.

Even without Brenda's support, Tyler had convinced himself that moving to Wyoming was what he wanted to do. His job became a drag. The days were long, and he no longer enjoyed his work. He wondered if he had the ability to build a home. The whole idea was exciting to him. He wanted badly to share his thoughts with Brenda, but he knew he didn't dare. She had to convince herself that this was a good idea, or she would blame Tyler forever if it didn't work out the way they planned. It was taking much more time for Brenda to come around than Tyler had expected, but he was convinced that one day she would accept the idea as a good one.

Chapter Fifteen

The phone rang in Tyler's office and he answered it on the second ring.

"Hello, Tyler. This is Tom Walton from Wyoming. Remember me? I ran into you up near Eagle Lake last summer. I was on horseback, looking for cattle."

Tyler was elated that Mr. Walton had remembered to call him. "Sure I remember you, Tom. What brings you to Chicago?"

Tom replied, "I told you I had a cousin here. Well, I finally decided to come visit him. I just wanted to get away from the ranch for a while, and I did have a little business to do here, so here I am."

"That's great, Tom. Welcome to Chicago. Will you have some time to get together with Brenda and I, for dinner?"

Tom hesitated for a moment before saying, "I don't want to be a pest. I just wanted to call and say 'hello.'"

"Come on, Tom, we would like to see you. I'd like to ask you some questions about Wyoming. I insist." Tom finally agreed to meet them for dinner the next evening. Tyler selected a nice steakhouse near Tom's hotel, and they agreed to meet there at seven o'clock.

Brenda and Tyler were glad to see Mr. Walton waiting for them when they arrived. He was very Western-looking in his gray pinstriped, Western-cut suit. His shirt, buttoned at the neck, sported a gold-inlaid silver clasp string tie. He had removed his hat and held it comfortably in front of him. He was a gentleman cowboy, boots and all.

The trio shook hands and visited briefly before being seated for dinner. Tom was quite a talker. The evening was both relaxing and enlightening. Brenda and Tyler anxiously listened as Tom answered their questions about life in Wyoming. They shuddered as he described in detail the long, cold winters. Tom sensed that their interest was more than casual. Tyler finally informed Tom that he, and perhaps Brenda, was giving serious thought to moving to the state. Tom was eager to find out what they planned to do and why they wanted to move there. Tyler told him that life in the city had been good to them, but they were now tired of the pace, and wanted to slow down and enjoy their lives a little.

Tom had a lot of information about what they could expect in the way of living accommodations, which interested Brenda more than Tyler. Tyler had convinced himself that he was capable of living in the wilderness, and that held more interest for him than accommodations in town. He wanted to get away from the busy city and try his skills at mountain living. Though he had no experience in this style of living, he was still confident that he could do it.

The three of them visited until closing time. Brenda and Tyler gave Tom a lift back to his hotel and wrote down his phone number and address in Wyoming. Tom volunteered to help in any way he could to make their move as smooth as possible. Brenda was now becoming convinced that she wanted to move to Wyoming. The visit with Mr. Walton was just what was needed to convince Brenda.

Tyler and Brenda agreed that the move would take place in the spring. Tyler would buy a four-wheel-drive pickup truck with a topper for the back, and they would pack all their belongings into the truck and drive up to Wyoming. It was really starting to sound like a fairy tale now. They could hardly wait.

There was a lot of work to do before leaving Chicago. Tyler must first resign from his job. He would carry out his plan for his portfolio, taking fifty thousand dollars in cash and investing the balance to yield a monthly income. Brenda's tasks were more domestic. She had to part with her furniture and find a home for her clothes—being in the women's fashion industry, she had acquired more clothing than she could ever use in Wyoming.

Things were coming together well. Tyler had informed his new boss of his intent to leave the firm. Though disappointed, Mr. Larson wished Tyler the best and told him he would be missed. Tyler informed Mr. Larson that he planned to head to Wyoming around the first of April. This would allow plenty of time for he and Brenda to get settled in to their new life before the long, cold, Wyoming winter arrived.

With each passing day, Brenda and Tyler got more excited. Apprehension prevented sleep most nights. Brenda was more worried than Tyler. After all, she was giving up her career and moving to Wyoming with a man she loved, but had no claim to. She wanted Tyler to marry her, but she knew that was not in his plans for the immediate future. Tyler had never mentioned marriage, but Brenda knew he loved her. She was willing to take her chances.

Brenda informed her employer of her plans. Her boss didn't handle the news of her leaving too well. In fact, she was told that the following Friday would be her last day. Brenda was prepared for this, and had purposely waited to inform her boss until the second week of March. She felt obligated to give two weeks notice, but wasn't too surprised when she was told that she wouldn't be needed past Friday of that week. She was considered a valuable employee when she was willing to work fifty to sixty hours a week, but now she was seen as a traitor.

Brenda spent the last three weeks prior to their departure doing things that needed to be done before leaving Chicago. She cashed in her retirement plan and paid off all her bills, then gave the remainder of the money to Tyler, to invest in some municipal bonds. Her furniture was sold to friends and acquaintances. Her clothing was donated to charitable organizations that were happy to get them.

Brenda moved in with Tyler, and they used her apartment to store the things they would take to Wyoming. When everything was consolidated, it looked like a lot of stuff to pack into the back of a pickup, but Tyler assured Brenda that he would make it fit.

Ads were placed in the paper and their vehicles were sold. Tyler now had to make a decision about which truck would best suit their needs. He purchased a white four-wheel-drive Ford with all the available accessories. The topper he selected was also white, with blue trim and sliding windows on each side. This vehicle would serve them well for the move, and also provide reliable transportation once they arrived at their new home.

There was no backing down now. The departure day had been selected. They would leave on Monday morning. Most of Sunday was spent loading the truck.

Tired as they were from loading the truck and taking care of the last details of their move, there was little sleep for Brenda and Tyler that night. Their apprehension was at its peak. Would the light of morning ever arrive?

Chapter
Sixteen

Brenda and Tyler were in the truck and headed out of town by eight o'clock. Tyler had plotted the entire trip to Jackson. They headed southwest out of Chicago and would catch Interstate 80 at Joliet, Illinois, then head west all the way to Rock Springs, Wyoming. From Rock Springs they would travel northwest, taking US 191 to Jackson. Tyler had calculated the mileage as just over fourteen hundred miles. He could have plotted a more direct route, saving them about two hundred miles of driving, but they would have to leave the interstate. With the load in the truck, Tyler felt it would be safer to stay on well-traveled roads, especially at this time of year. Tyler had planned to travel to Lincoln, Nebraska, the first day, about five hundred miles away. The next day they would travel to Cheyenne, Wyoming—another five hundred miles. The last day of travel would cover four hundred miles, putting them in Jackson, Wyoming.

The first day of travel was exciting for Brenda and Tyler. The passion of their dreams for the past year was about to become reality. The truck handled the load well and enabled them to travel at the speed limit most of the time. The travelers were right on schedule, arriving in Lincoln, Nebraska, before dark.

Their second day of travel was overcast and gloomy. After a nice breakfast, Tyler filled the thermos with hot coffee, and the travelers continued west on Interstate 80. Travel slowed as it began to rain. The highway was loaded with eighteen-wheelers, and trying to pass the cumbersome giants was nearly impossible. The windshield wipers couldn't keep up with the rain that sprayed from the rear wheels of the large trucks. Tyler was forced to drive slowly.

After they ate lunch at a truck stop, the rain abated and the sun began to shine. Travel speed picked up and they arrived in Cheyenne, Wyoming, just as daylight waned. The temperature had dropped below freezing and light rain was starting to fall again. Ice crystals began to form, sticking to the windshield. Brenda and Tyler checked into a nice motel just as the roads were starting to get slick. The wind was picking up and blizzard warnings had been issued—a common occurrence in Wyoming in early April. Brenda and Tyler were not too happy about the weather, but they knew they'd better get used to it. They were now in the midst of a good old Wyoming spring blizzard.

The next morning found the travelers still in the midst of the blizzard. Nearly twelve inches of snow had fallen during the night, and the wind continued to blow at about thirty miles an hour. The interstate was still closed. It appeared they would be spending some time in Cheyenne—three more days, to be exact. The motel had a small bar, which was loaded with travelers by mid-morning and buzzed with chatter until well after midnight. There was nothing else to do. One couldn't leave the motel, and after a few hours of reading, the soul gets restless. The bar's business was booming.

Brenda and Tyler met some very interesting people in the bar, some of whom they would never forget, and some of whom they wanted to forget before morning. It was an interesting way to spend a few days, but they were definitely ready for a change of scenery.

On the third morning, the sun was shining at last. The wind was still blowing, and the storm front had passed; the snowplows were starting to move around the little town. The interstate was still closed. The road from Cheyenne to Laramie had huge snow drifts across it, and the plows would not have the road open until some-time the next day. Brenda and Tyler were able to start their truck and drive it to a small theater in town. A movie was a welcome change in the boring routine of the stranded travelers. It wasn't an excellent movie, but it didn't matter much to Brenda and Tyler. They were away from the motel, and they were able to drive. It was amazing how a blizzard could make little things like getting out and seeing a movie seem so fabulous.

The interstate was open the next morning, and the travelers were able to proceed with their trip. Travel was still slow and dan-gerous. The wind blew hard, and the snow blowing across the road made visibility almost nonexistent. It was just a little over forty miles to Laramie, the next town on their route. They were about halfway there when Tyler pulled into a rest area. He needed to remove the ice and snow that had built up under the fenders of the truck. By prodding around with a tire iron, he was successful in loosening most of the ice and snow. He could now steer the truck without the tires rubbing the ice.

Tyler decided to use the rest room while they were there. He opened the door to enter the men's room and was greeted by a small, bouncing brown puppy, which yipped with excitement when it saw him. Tyler leaned down to pat the lonesome stranger. Apparently, someone had left the puppy behind by mistake. Perhaps someone had just dropped it off, thinking that someone else would take pity on the little animal and give it a home. When Tyler was ready to leave, the puppy whined and barked, making it clear that it didn't want to be left behind. Tyler picked up the little stranger and walked back to the truck, where Brenda was waiting.

"Look what I found in the men's room," he said. "Someone left him or abandoned him."

Brenda, having a soft spot in her heart for small animals, took the puppy from Tyler's arms and cuddled it in her lap. "Oh, Tyler, we can't leave this little puppy here. It will starve, or freeze to death." The puppy seemed content with Brenda's affection. It licked her and whined to show its appreciation.

Brenda and Tyler now had a traveling companion. The puppy was very young—only a few weeks old. It couldn't survive on its own, so Tyler and Brenda decided they must take it with them. The puppy was mostly brown, with a black tip on its tail and a black patch around its right eye. After a quick check, Tyler determined that the puppy was a boy. What would they name their new friend? they wondered.

The road was clearing, and driving was much safer. As the truck slowly descended the small mountain range, the snow started to melt and run from the roadside. It was a welcome relief to find a dry highway.

The travelers arrived in Laramie, Wyoming, and left the interstate to gas the truck and buy some food for their hungry little companion. They left the puppy in the truck and went to grab a bite to eat. When they returned, the puppy was curled up, sleeping soundly in the seat. What a cute little friend and companion they had found!

Back on the interstate, Brenda fed the puppy, holding it like a small baby. The puppy was lucky to have found them.

As they continued to travel west they searched their minds, trying to come up with a good name for their newfound friend. They took turns picking names. Finally, after about a hundred miles of

picking and choosing, Brenda came up with the name "Bud." She
had a puppy as a child whose name was Bud, and she had always
liked the name. Tyler reached over, rubbed the little pup on the
nose, and said, "Bud it is. I like it." Bud slept for most of the remainder of the trip to Rock Springs, Wyoming.

In Rock Springs, Tyler fueled the truck and took Bud for a
short walk. The travelers were tired and decided to spend the night.
The rest of the trip to Jackson Hole would be completed the next
morning.

Tyler, Brenda, and Bud left the motel early. They passed
through the little town of Pinedale shortly after ten o'clock. The
scenery was beautiful. The snow-covered mountains stood behind
beautiful green meadows, which were covered with pockets of colorful aspens. Small, clear creeks made paths through the meadows
and provided water for the countless cattle that were grazing on the
endless supply of grass. The mountains gave Tyler and Brenda a
warm, welcome feeling.

The rest of the trip to Jackson, through the Hoback Canyon and
the Gros Ventre Mountains, was slow and enjoyable. The scenery
was gorgeous, and the weather was perfect. The sky was blue, and
not a cloud could be seen. It was a perfect Wyoming spring day.
Even Bud seemed to enjoy it.

The travelers arrived in Jackson Hole at lunch time and
checked into a small motel near the edge of town, overlooking the
beautiful Snake River. Tyler walked over to the motel lobby, purchased a local paper, and began searching for a house to rent.
Ideally, they would like to find a small place away from town, so Bud
would have a place to run and play. There were three houses listed
in the paper which seemed to fit their needs. Tyler made some
phone calls and scheduled appointments to look at two that had not
been rented. One of the appointments was the following morning.

They found the first place easily, as it was located just off the
highway along the Snake River, about three miles from their motel.
It needed a lot of work, and was much too small. It had a great view,
but they were not willing to sacrifice good living conditions for a
nice view. The rest of the first day was spent driving around looking for other places that might not be listed in the paper. They
found nothing else to look at that day.

The next morning they drove up to look at the second house,
which was located about two miles up a rocky dirt road along a little

stream. It sat back in a small, wooded area and was difficult to see from the road. It was a natural log house with a detached, two-car garage. It was fully furnished, and had a small, fenced yard in the rear, which would be perfect for Bud. The interior had a small, cozy living room with a fireplace. There were two bedrooms and a nice large kitchen with all the appliances, including a washer and dryer. This house would be great for the three of them. They rented it and began moving in that afternoon.

Finding a suitable place had proven to be much easier that they had anticipated. They had gotten lucky. The house had been occupied by a widow who had fallen and broken her hip. The family decided she could no longer live alone, and moved her into a retirement home. Her brother, who was renting the house, gave Tyler the option of using the furniture or storing it in the room above the garage. Tyler and Brenda felt that the home was comfortably furnished and decided to leave everything in its place, except for a couple of storage trunks in one of the bedrooms, which Tyler moved into the garage.

In a few days the couple had settled into their new home and were ready to relax and enjoy life. The timber from the moose encounter was placed over the fireplace on two nails that had once held an old gun belonging to the widow's husband. Tyler and Brenda could now spend time exploring and enjoying their new home and wonderful Wyoming.

Chapter

Seventeen

Summer in Jackson Hole was enjoyable for the three new residents. Tyler was quickly learning to relax in the style of Jackson natives. Fishing seemed to be the pastime that he enjoyed the most. He was able to take Brenda and Bud along, and he was actually getting to be an accomplished fisherman. Fly-fishing is not the easiest thing for a novice fisherman to do, but with a lot of practice, Tyler developed his skills until he was quite proficient.

When Tyler wasn't fishing, he was painting. His painting skills were starting to exceed the amateur stage. Brenda was amazed at how easy painting was for Tyler. He could put his brush on the canvas and capture his subject in great detail, almost as well as a professional could.

One afternoon while Tyler was painting, Brenda went into town. She stopped by the ladies' apparel shop to visit with the owner, whom she had met while working for the clothing company. The owner offered Brenda a job at the shop. She was flattered, but wasn't quite ready to go back to work. She was still enjoying her time with Tyler and Bud. When the weather got cold and they could no longer spend their days outdoors, she might think about the job offer more seriously. Right now, working was not a priority, but she did enjoy the comfort of knowing she could have a job if she wanted one. She might need it later.

One day, while Tyler was in town picking up some painting supplies, he decided to stop by a local bar for a drink. The bar was not too busy; it was occupied by only a few "natives," who were sipping beer and discussing the dreadful tourist traffic. Tyler nursed his drink and visited casually with the bartender. The heavy wooden door creaked open, and Tyler was surprised to see Tom Walton entering the bar.

"Hey, Tom," Tyler said. "Sit down and let me buy you a drink."

Tom was happy to see Tyler, and could hardly believe that he was finally a Wyoming resident. Tyler and Tom visited for quite some time, and Tyler accepted an invitation to travel up to Tom's ranch on Saturday with Brenda and Bud for a cookout. Tom sketched a map of the route to his ranch on the back of a bar napkin, which Tyler stuffed in his pocket before leaving to drive home.

Brenda was happy to hear of their invitation to visit the Box W Ranch. "What time on Saturday are we expected at the Box W?" she asked.

"Tom said we could come up anytime in the afternoon. I thought it might be fun to get there early. Perhaps we could talk Tom into loaning us some horses for a little ride around his ranch."

Brenda liked this idea, and they agreed to depart shortly after lunch on Saturday. It would likely take an hour or so to drive up and locate the ranch.

Bud was growing like a weed. He was now a little over three months old, and was quite a pal. It was apparent that he would not be a large dog–Tyler estimated that he would be about the size of a small chow. Bud stood about fifteen inches tall and weighed approximately twenty pounds. He loved to ride in the truck, especially in the back.

On Saturday, Bud climbed into the back of the truck, and they left for their visit to the Waltons' Box W Ranch. Bud barked at every squirrel and chipmunk he saw along the way. He stood on his hind legs and looked directly into the stiff breeze created by the speed of the truck; he loved it.

Tom was sitting in a large rocking chair on the front porch of his beautiful log home when the trio arrived. Immediately, Mrs. Walton came to the door of the ranch house to meet their visitors.

"Tyler and Brenda, meet my wife Betty," Tom said. "This is Tyler and Brenda, who I've been telling you about, from Chicago."

Betty reached out, shook Tyler's hand, and said, "Welcome to the Box W, and welcome to Wyoming."

Tyler leaned over, patted Bud on the head, and said, "This is Bud. We found him at a rest area on our trip out here from Chicago."

Betty invited the visitors to join them on the porch, then went inside to get some iced tea. She was a pretty lady–very attractive for her age–and was dressed typically in Levi's, a Western shirt, and a pair of boots. Her hair was pulled back and tied into a ponytail that nearly reached her shoulders. She appeared to be a few years younger than Tom—Tyler estimated she was near forty-five.

The couples visited on the porch for some time, enjoying their iced tea before Tyler mentioned the horseback ride. Tom and Betty agreed that it was an excellent idea.

"It would be nice if the four of us could take a ride," Betty said. Tom agreed, and he and Tyler went to saddle the horses.

They rode with Tyler and Tom leading the way; Betty and Brenda followed close behind. The ride was relaxing and beautiful. They followed a nice trail though the trees along a babbling brook, heading in an easterly direction. Tom pulled his horse to a stop on a high bluff overlooking a large valley and pointed to a lake in the distance. He broke the silence by saying, "Eagle Lake, remember it? The two of you were looking at that lake when I rode up on you last summer."

Tyler looked at Tom and said, "Sure do, Tom. Do you remember it, Brenda?"

Brenda scanned the area with an expression of disbelief and responded, "Yes, I do, but where were we, Tyler?"

Tom pointed to a distant bluff to the right. "That's it over there. The two of you were standing on that bluff. My place runs from the road to town to the edge of the lake, down near the far end."

Tyler was surprised that the Box W Ranch was so large. It encompassed nearly ten thousand acres.

After admiring the view for a short time, they turned the horses around and headed back to the ranch. Bud had been running alongside them, exploring every little bush and rock, and he was getting tired and hot. He'd regularly leave the trail to lie in the cool water of a nearby brook, then he'd run to catch up with the horses.

When they arrived back at the ranch, the horses were unsaddled in the barn, and Tyler helped Tom curry them before turning them loose in the corral to be fed. Betty and Brenda went to the house to prepare the dinner of steaks cooked in an open pit, cowboy beans, fresh lettuce salad, and homemade bread.

Tyler and Tom enjoyed a couple of bourbons while the women sipped wine and finished the dinner preparations. Tom was designated to cook the steaks. The fire had been started and had burned down just about enough when Tom placed the steaks on the sizzling grate. There was no question that Tom knew what he was doing. The steaks were the best Brenda and Tyler had ever had.

After dinner they returned to the porch for a little liqueur and more visiting. They had just sat down when they heard Bud barking in the trees behind the barn. It was almost dark, and they were unable to see what was upsetting the excited dog. Tyler called, but Bud didn't come. Then, he began howling as if he was beaten with a club. He arrived at the porch, whining and crying wildly.

"Damn," Tom said. "Poor little bastard found a porcupine." Tom grabbed Bud and pinned him to the floor with his knees, straddling the howling dog, who had gotten a mouthful of quills from the culprit. Tom reached for the small leather pouch on his belt and retrieved a pair of pliers. Tyler later learned that pliers in such pouches were standard equipment for ranchers. Tom asked Tyler to hold Bud's head as he pulled the quills from the dog's face. Tom had obviously done this before. He grabbed each quill and forcefully yanked it out. Bud was in severe pain, and Tom was not a gentle doctor by any stretch of the imagination.

The quill of a porcupine is barbed, and almost impossible to pull out. One can only tear them from the flesh like pulling a fishhook out the way it went in. The quill of a porcupine has been known to kill its victims. Contrary to belief, a porcupine can't shoot its quills, but when pressure is applied to the exposed, pointed end, it quickly penetrates the flesh. It continues to work its way deeper, and many times it will penetrate a vital organ.

As Tom pulled the quills, he commented that the porcupine is a strange animal.

It is seldom aggressive, he said, and actually has a quite docile nature. When confronted with danger, a porcupine will roll into a ball and lie motionless, much like an opossum. Experienced handlers can pick them up quite easily without getting hurt by brushing the quills from the front of the animal to the rear and grabbing the creature while the quills are down, avoiding pressure on the pointed ends. Once the porcupine is lifted in the air, it is harmless and helpless. Tom also mentioned that a porcupine will seldom bite.

Bud had been lucky. He had gotten only eight of the quills embedded in his face. When the last quill was extracted, Bud lay very still on the porch, in severe pain. Tom went to the barn, got some horse-cut disinfectant, and applied a generous amount to Bud's wounds. The poor dog was hurting.

Brenda was suffering as much as Bud from the whole ordeal. Betty felt bad that she and Tom hadn't warned them about the porcupines in the area. Brenda and Tyler assured her that it wasn't her fault and that Bud would be fine.

Tom gently patted the little dog on the head. He turned to Tyler and said, "There are two things that one must learn to respect in the wilderness of Wyoming—porcupines and bears. Those two varmints always win. Never cross them, and give them plenty of space—as much as they want. Remember that as long as you live in Wyoming."

A short time later, Tyler and Brenda decided it was time to go. Bud's encounter with the porcupine had caused a great day to turn sad. They thanked the Waltons for their hospitality and the relaxing horse ride. They all agreed to get together again soon. Tyler and Brenda put Bud into the front seat of the truck and started home. The little dog lay in Brenda's lap and whimpered for most of the trip. Once home, Tyler carried Bud inside and placed him on a blanket beside their bed. They checked on Bud every hour or so for most of the night. He seemed to be doing fine, though he wasn't resting well.

The next morning, Bud's face was quite swollen, and he wasn't very mobile. Tyler and Brenda loaded him into the truck and took him to see the veterinarian, who carefully examined him. He advised Brenda and Tyler that Bud had been lucky. He would need a lot of rest, and must be given antibiotics to prevent infection.

Before they left, the vet commented, "With a porcupine, a dog never learns his lesson. In all probability, the next time Bud comes across a porcupine, the same thing will happen. There's something about a dog that makes it think it can win the fight. A dog will tangle with a porcupine every time it comes across one. Few dogs ever learn to leave them alone. It's sad, but true."

The next few days were spent nursing Bud back to health. Tyler spent some time painting and fishing. Bud showed little interest in accompanying Tyler, who missed having his little buddy on the riverbank with him. Bud was like a son to him.

It was about a week before Bud acted like he wanted to play. He was still fairly inactive and slept a lot of the time. Brenda and Tyler were happy when Bud started running around the house. He was finally feeling better, returning to his normal, mischievous self.

It was a peaceful, relaxing summer for the three of them, with no social or business pressures. They fished, Tyler painted, and all three of them went exploring whenever the notion hit them.

Fall was just around the corner, and the mornings and evenings were getting cool. Temperatures often fell below freezing, and the mountains were starting to sport their winter blankets of beautiful white snow.

Then, Indian summer arrived in Wyoming; it was beautiful, with bright sunny days and cool evenings. As it often does, it lasted until the first of November, when the droves of hunters arrived to make their kills of the plentiful game. Jackson Hole was a popular hunting area, and hunters came from as far away as California and Texas. Non-resident hunting licenses were allocated by a drawing. Applicants must send in applications in the spring, and the drawing is held in July. Lucky license recipients would be notified by mail shortly thereafter, giving them ample time to plan their trips.

The tourist season had drawn to a close, and the town was now crammed with hunters. After hunting season the skiers would arrive, and they would be in and out of the town until late March. The Jackson ski slopes are advertised throughout the world for their fine skiing. Brenda enjoyed skiing, but Tyler, not being an experienced skier, didn't want to risk potential injury by participating in the popular sport. He did concede to skiing on the more subtle, gentle slopes. Tyler went with Brenda to be accommodating, but he didn't enjoy it that much. Brenda wanted to be with Tyler every moment of every day, and going skiing without him didn't hold much attraction for her. They spent a lot of time just being together and cultivating their love, which had grown into a beautiful romance.

Christmastime in the mountains was beautiful. The snow had fallen two feet deep around their home. Bud loved it, running and playing in it until he was exhausted.

Brenda and Tyler kept the Christmas season very simple and old-fashioned. No expensive gifts were purchased. Their gifts to each other were mainly things that they had made. Tyler presented Brenda with one of his favorite wildlife paintings, framed with aspen. Brenda gave Tyler a nice wool sweater that she had knitted. Bud got a leather collar, hand-tooled with an inscription of his name. He wore his new collar proudly.

Brenda and Tyler budgeted their expenditures well, and the only money spent was for rent, food, and necessities. They were living comfortably, and their money source seemed adequate. Tyler occasionally phoned to check on his portfolio. It too was doing just fine, and the interest checks for the bonds were arriving regularly. Things were going well for them.

Tom and Betty Walton had become their good friends. The two couples would meet occasionally for dinner or get together at one of their homes for cards and conversation. One evening, after dinner at a local restaurant, Tyler sprung an idea on Tom.

He asked, "Tom, would you be interested in selling me a small parcel of land over by Eagle Lake? I have a plan. I would like to build a home there—a cabin."

The idea took Tom by surprise. "Build a home?" Tom responded. "Clear out there? How do you propose to get back and forth? There's no roads up to that lake."

Tyler spent the next hour or so telling Tom about his plan. He would buy an all-terrain vehicle, commonly referred to as an "ATV," for summer travel, and a snowmobile for winter travel. Tyler had given the idea a lot of thought, and Tom was impressed with the details he had worked out. "How much land do you want to buy? Enough to raise livestock, or just a home site?" Tom asked.

"Just enough for a home site. Say, a couple of acres, or whatever you would be willing to sell."

Tom placed his right hand around his chin and sat in silence, staring into space. After a time he said, "I'm not crazy about the idea, but if you would be willing to sign an agreement that I had the first right of refusal should you decide to sell, I would consider it."

Brenda was surprised. Tyler had never mentioned this idea to her before. She was now quite certain that Tyler had lost his mind. Perhaps the abundance of idle time has caused Tyler's mind to go dormant, to mold and get stale, or something, she giggled to herself.

As he continued to talk about his plan, Brenda realized that he was serious. This scared the hell out of her—she was petrified.

Before leaving the restaurant that evening, Tyler had gotten a commitment from Tom that he would sell some property—two acres for two thousand dollars. The two men would head up to Eagle Lake in early spring and measure off land adjoining the lake. This would give Tyler adequate room to build his cabin. Tyler agreed not to fence the site, at Tom's insistence. He also agreed to pay the surveyor to come up and stake the property boundaries. Tyler and Tom shook hands on the deal, and the Waltons headed back to the Box W Ranch. Tyler felt like he had accomplished the deal of a lifetime. His own land, near a glacier lake in Wyoming—it was a dream come true for him. He spent the rest of the winter drawing up the plans for his log cabin, making endless lists of the materials he would need. Before spring arrived, Tyler had purchased a four-wheel-drive ATV and a little trailer to pull behind it for hauling the materials up to the site.

Tyler also purchased a dependable snowmobile to use during the winter. Brenda was totally astounded when she learned that he not only planned to have the three of them live in the cabin, but he also expected them to spend the winter there!

Tyler spent a great deal of time reading books on how to build a cabin and on structure engineering. He had never tackled a job of this complexity, but he was confident that he could build a warm, safe, comfortable place. He shopped almost daily for the equipment and supplies that he would need, including a generator for the power tools and lights at night, a large iron stove for cooking and winter heating, bags of concrete for building the foundation and fireplace, a wheelbarrow for hauling rocks and mixing concrete, and metal roofing for the cabin. Nearly every imaginable hand tool was purchased. Tyler would return in the truck nearly every day and unload his purchases into the garage, which was much too full to accommodate the truck any longer. Tyler checked his extensive list every evening, crossing off the items that had been purchased that day—nails, a stovepipe, bolts and nuts, screws, insulation, doors, windows, big saws, little saws. The list went on and on.

Tyler was nearing the end of his list, and spring was just around the corner. He would now contact the surveyor and identify his little parcel of land. Building would begin immediately after the surveying was complete and he had paid Mr. Walton for the land.

Brenda was in shock. It was unbelievable, the way Tyler relentlessly pursued the project. Once he had made up his mind, he was like a determined, mad bull. Through all of Tyler's enthusiasm, Brenda had remained supportive, and even pretended to be excited about the project. She did this because she loved Tyler, and had nothing to do with building the wilderness castle that Tyler dreamed about.

Chapter Eighteen

Tyler loaded his ATV in his truck and put Bud in the front seat beside him. He was on his way to meet the surveyor at the Box W Ranch that morning so they could stake the two acres of land that he would be purchasing from Tom. Bud was grown now, and had become Tyler's sidekick. Tyler couldn't go anywhere in the truck without him.

The surveyor had already arrived at the Box W and was visiting with Tom Walton when Tyler and Bud pulled the truck into the yard. The surveyor introduced himself as Joe Riley. After a short visit with Tyler, he loaded his transit and several maps into a wooden box that was conveniently mounted on the back of his ATV. It took only a few moments for Tyler to unload his ATV and he, too, was ready to go. Tom pointed out on the map the location of the land he thought would best satisfy Tyler's needs, and plotted a trail that would likely be the best route of travel. Tyler straddled his ATV and called for Bud to join him. The dog jumped up and sat on the gas tank between Tyler's legs, ready to ride.

The trip up to Eagle Lake was a little rough and slow, as there was still a lot of snow in the mountains. A few detours had to be made to get around some large drifts that had filled the chosen trail and made it impassable. It was a scenic ride, and the ATVs handled the snow and steep inclines with ease.

Tyler, Bud, and Joe arrived at the still-frozen lake near its lower end. Joe got off his ATV and walked out on the lake to check the ice, which he found was still firmly frozen and safe to ride on. They proceeded with caution, picking their way along the edge of the lake. Travel on the lake was quick and smooth. The six-inch snow cover on the frozen lake was perfect for riding.

They rode the ATVs up the lake, nearly to its end. Joe pulled his machine up on a snow-covered beach, beside a stand of mature aspens. Behind the aspens were miles of tall lodgepole pines, which Tyler was studying with great interest. The pines would be the main structure of his home, and he was happy to find a limitless source of the fine trees so close to the chosen home site.

Joe studied the map for quite some time before he turned to Tyler and asked, "Where do you want your acreage to start? Select a starting point for me, and I can go to work."

Tyler walked a few steps up the beach and stopped to look at the mountains and trees. After a short time he picked a spot.

"Right here. I'd like to have one of the corner stakes here, and I want about eight hundred feet of lakefront. Then, take as much land back away from the lake as you need to give me a two-acre parcel."

Joe immediately began to drive a steel stake marked with a bright orange ribbon into the still-frozen ground. He then measured eight hundred feet down the edge of the lake and drove in the second stake. He set his transit and began to plot the points of reference on his map. Bud spent his time running and exploring the surroundings. Tyler took the opportunity to snap a few pictures of the area to share with Brenda. It was a gorgeous site, tranquil and beautiful.

Joe drove in the fourth stake, then attached longer wooden stakes and more orange flags. The surveying completed, the two men and Bud crawled on their ATVs and headed back to the Box W Ranch.

Tom met them as they pulled into the yard. "All done?" he asked.

"Surveyed and staked, ready for your inspection," Joe replied. Tom advised them that he would ride up the next morning and check the stakes to make certain the site met with his approval. All that would be left to do after that would be to go to the courthouse, register the sale, and pay Tom, and the building site would belong to Tyler.

Tyler loaded his ATV in the truck and put Bud in the cab, then drove home. They arrived just as Brenda was setting the table for dinner. She had prepared a nice beef stew for Tyler—one of his favorite meals. They had a restful and enjoyable dinner, which was accompanied by a few glasses of wine. After the dishes were washed, Tyler spread the map on the table and showed Brenda the general location of the home site he had selected. She was anxious to see the pictures Tyler had taken that afternoon.

Tyler became more intense than ever with his efforts to purchase the materials he would need to build the home. One of his last purchases was a large wall tent with a floor that would be used for living quarters while the cabin was being built. He also purchased another large tent for storing the tools and equipment that needed protection from the weather. It seemed as though he had thought of everything.

His next project was to rent a large truck to haul the equipment up to the Box W Ranch. He had made arrangements with Tom to store the building tools and materials in the barn until they could be moved up to the building site.

Several trips were required to get all the materials to the barn. As best he could, Tyler arranged them in the order that they would be hauled to the site. With all the materials in the barn, he loaded the trailer with the tents and the tools that would be used to clear the building site. After considerable thought, he decided to buy another ATV and trailer. They could use the extra vehicle for transportation, and it would be nice to haul two loads of materials at a time. This ATV was a little larger than the first he had purchased, and had more pulling capability. He then purchased another trailer. Tyler estimated it would take as many as twenty trips from the Box W Ranch to haul their supplies to the building site. The extra vehicle and trailer would make the job much quicker.

Brenda and Tyler had decided to keep the rental home. It would provide a place to stay when they came to town, and would prevent them from having to take all of their personal belongings up to the building site. They realized the whole thing could turn sour, and keeping a home to come back to would be wise. Their landlord agreed to keep an eye on the place during their absence.

The couple was now ready to head up to Eagle Lake and start their new home. Brenda was still uneasy at the thought of it, with all the unknowns they would likely encounter. However, Tyler remained confident that he possessed the skills to build the cabin and survive in the wilderness. They would soon find out whether or not he was right.

Tom phoned Brenda and Tyler to inform them that they were the proud owners of a two-acre parcel of land on Eagle Lake, and wished them luck in their venture. Tyler found it hard to sleep. The excitement was really starting to build within him. He wanted to get up to Eagle Lake and get started. His mind was occupied with never-ending thoughts of things that he might have forgotten. How long would it take to build the cabin? Did he have enough knowledge to do what he was attempting to do? Would he like living up at Eagle Lake? Would Brenda like it up there? The thoughts went on and on, but it was too late to change his mind now.

Chapter Nineteen

The time arrived for moving the construction equipment to the building site. With the trailers loaded and plenty of extra fuel for the ATVs, Tyler, Brenda, and Bud headed for Eagle Lake. The trail was mostly free of snow now, and the going was surprisingly easy. The time required for the first trip was a little over two hours—not bad, considering the muddy trails and the loads they were carrying.

Eagle Lake was still frozen when they arrived. However, it was starting to thaw a little; it appeared to be at least a couple of weeks away from being a lake again. The building site was just as Tyler had remembered it. The work would now begin.

The first project was to erect the sleeping tent and get it ready for occupancy. Next, the equipment tent was erected. The equipment tent was larger than the sleeping tent, but didn't have a floor. It could also double as a cooking tent if the weather became inclement, as it likely would from time to time.

The trailers were unloaded and the tools and supplies were stowed in the larger tent. Tyler fired up the chain saw and began to fell trees where the cabin would be erected, among them eight or ten aspens that were six to eight inches in diameter. The aspen wood was soft, and the cutting was easy. Once the trees were down, Tyler cut the trunks and limbs into small pieces and placed them neatly in a stack for future use as firewood. It would be some time before the wood dried enough to be burned.

Brenda erected the cots and rolled out the sleeping bags while Tyler worked. After moving her cot as close as possible to Tyler's, she tidied the tent and fashioned a makeshift kitchen, which was quite functional. She then prepared a dinner of fried eggs, bacon, and fried potatoes on the camp stove, which worked surprisingly well.

Tyler poured a stiff shot of bourbon before sitting down to eat the meal that Brenda had prepared. After the first few bites he looked at her and asked, "Why is it that food tastes so much better in the mountains than it does in town?"

Much was accomplished the first day. Brenda and Tyler were ready for their sleeping bags early. The temperature still dropped very low at night, and Bud curled up at the foot of Tyler's sleeping bag for warmth. There wasn't a sound to be heard as they lay snuggled together, except a slight breeze rustling through the branches of the trees. Though exhausted from the work they had done that day, their excitement made sleeping difficult. The quiet environment was uncanny, almost frightening. Brenda was uncomfortable, listening intently for sounds of potential danger. Bud was the only quick sleeper—good ol' Bud, the guard dog.

The next morning, serious work began. After Tyler drove stakes into the ground and ran a taut string between them, the perimeter of the foundation was established. Tyler then hauled several loads of rocks, four to six inches in diameter, to be used for the foundation. Concrete was mixed in the wheelbarrow to cement the rocks in place, providing a firm footing for the cabin.

Several trips were made back to the barn to haul needed materials to the building site. The bottoms of the trailers were loaded with the bagged concrete, and lighter materials were placed on top, including the wheelbarrow, the electric generator, shovels, a rake, and a hoe. The hoe was needed to mix the concrete. The sand from the beach was perfect for blending with the concrete to make the cement, and the lake water for mixing the concrete was readily available once Tyler had chopped a hole in the ice with an ax. Brenda mixed the concrete while Tyler meticulously put the rocks in place, forming a perfectly level foundation for the cabin structure. To make the proper mix, five buckets of sand were combined with one bucket of concrete. The last ingredient added was the water.

It took Tyler and Brenda the better part of three days to complete the foundation. Once completed, the concrete would need a little time to cure. A couple of days would be adequate.

While waiting, Tyler started cutting the timbers to construct the floor supports. The floor supports would not need to be large, but a lot of effort must be made to find good, straight poles. If the poles selected were not straight, the finished floor would not be level. Tyler spent a lot of time searching for the perfect logs before dragging them to the building site with the ATV. The poles were meticulously cut, placed in position, and anchored to the foundation with more concrete. Tyler also anchored the middle of each pole to the ground, to keep the floor from giving under stress. He had remembered all the important points from the books he read. So far so good.

Next, timber for the walls had to be found. Tyler was successful in finding some dead trees to make the wall members. Standing dead timber is perfect for this purpose, as downed trees are normally wet and prone to rot quickly. Also, once down, termites attack almost immediately and weaken the wood.

Each timber needed to be shaved of bark, cut to length, notched, and placed on the foundation. The preparation of each log was time-consuming and tedious. Each one had to fit perfectly, or there would be large gaps between them, allowing cold air to enter in the winter.

Tyler was meticulous in selecting and preparing each log for use. It took a lot of time, but his efforts would be worthwhile. He generously caulked between each layer of logs with concrete, and taught Brenda to use a putty knife to cover the concrete with latex caulking to fill the small holes. Once dried, the concrete and caulking would hold the logs in place for several years and provide a nearly airtight seal.

Tyler had almost finished the walls when Brenda asked, "Tyler, it's starting to look great, but what about the doors and windows? Aren't we going to have any?"

He chuckled and kissed her on the cheek. "Sure we are. But we don't cut the holes for the doors and windows until the walls are completed."

Brenda nodded her head and smiled as if she understood, but she had no idea how that was going to work.

It was time for a break. A shower and a meal at a restaurant sounded great to the two tired workers. Tyler, Brenda, and Bud secured their camp, crawled on their ATVs and headed to town. The warm shower and soft bed at their home in town were wonderful that night. They spent a few days there resting up. Materials that Tyler had overlooked or miscalculated the quantities of were purchased. Tyler also bought a handgun and a rifle. He had felt a little insecure up at the cabin site without protection. Spring was in full swing, and the threat of bears was now a concern. Tyler didn't know if he could shoot a bear, but he wanted a gun just in case one came nosing around the building site.

Tyler, Brenda, and Bud returned to the cabin site to find the supply tent in shambles. Something had ripped the side of the tent and entered. It looked as though a bomb had exploded in a Salvation Army warehouse. Was it an animal looking for food? The intruder had completely wrecked the tent, scattering tools and building supplies everywhere. After close examination, Tyler found some footprints. They were quite large, and Tyler was certain they had been made by an inquisitive bear. Brenda and Tyler were glad they had not been there when the intruder came to visit. They must be extremely careful. If the bear had found food, and they were confident that it had, it most likely would return for more.

After a few more days of work, the exterior walls were complete, and the structure was starting to resemble a cabin. The next major undertaking was building the roof. It had to be erected with enough slope to prevent the snow from piling up. A load of snow on the roof could cause the entire structure to collapse, a serious consideration for homes built in Wyoming. Metal would work best, as snow wouldn't stick to it easily and would slide off once the sun warmed it.

Tyler had planned for this, purchasing galvanized metal sheets for the roof of the cabin. He had also purchased three-quarter-inch exterior-grade plywood for the sub-roof. The supports were put in place and the plywood sub-roof was firmly nailed on. Next, felt roofing paper was rolled out and tacked to the entire surface, on top of the plywood. The metal sheets were put in place, and black roofing tar was applied under each seam in the metal to prevent possible leaks. The roof, now complete, was not pretty, but it was quite functional.

Building the floor was the next project. It, too, was covered with three-quarter-inch exterior-grade plywood. Before the final layer of flooring was applied, Tyler cut a four-by-four-foot hole in the floor and dug a hole six feet deep beneath it. He then framed and sided the hole before pouring a concrete floor in it. This space would be used for food storage. The storage area would remain cool in warm weather and wouldn't freeze in the winter. It would be accessible from inside the cabin through a trapdoor, which he cut and fit over the opening. Tyler then built shelves down one side of the storage area and hung a small ladder from the top, against the other side.

The following day, Tyler applied the rolled roofing felt to the plywood sub-floor. The finished floor of the cabin would be three-by-twelve oiled planks. The plank floor would require little maintenance and would provide a good solid base.

The cabin was nearly ready for occupancy, which was none too soon for Brenda. The arrival of the bear had caused her a lot of worry. She didn't sleep well at night, and every little noise got her heart pounding. Neither Tyler nor Brenda had ever seen a bear in the wild. She wasn't looking forward to it.

The cabin was now ready for doors and windows. The structure would have one large entrance in the front, facing the lake, and a smaller door on the downwind, kitchen side of the cabin. Tyler marked the selected locations for the doors and easily cut the openings with his chain saw. The doors were solid hardwood and pre-hung in their casings, which made the installation process quite simple once the holes had been cut.

The double-pane windows were installed using the same procedure. The plans called for one large window and one small window on the front wall of the cabin, two small windows on each of the side walls, and one small window on the rear wall. The cabin was now ready for Brenda to start applying linseed oil to the exterior, to preserve the wood. The dry logs readily soaked up the oil, and two coats were required to properly seal and weatherproof the cabin.

Late one evening, as darkness approached, Brenda noticed that Bud was gone. After repeated calls and whistles, the dog still didn't show. Tyler was quite concerned. He finished putting his tools away, grabbed a lantern, and went searching for Bud, insisting that Brenda stay at the camp.

Tyler walked down the edge of the lake, whistling and calling. It wasn't until he was nearly ready to return to camp that he heard a whimpering sound from a small thicket of nearby bushes. He cautiously approached the bush, and spotted Bud. The dog was lying in a pool of blood, trying to raise his head. He had bled enough to make him weak, and was helpless. Tyler leaned over and gently patted Bud on the head, talking softly to him while surveying the damage. He seemed to be bleeding from a gash on his side. Closer inspection revealed that there were two parallel gashes along the wounded dog's rib cage. His bottom jaw quivered as Tyler gently rubbed his head. Tyler removed his jacket and covered the suffering animal. He carefully picked him up and headed back down the lake shore to the cabin.

By the time Tyler arrived with Bud, Brenda was a wreck. Tyler placed the injured dog on his cot to examine the wounds in more detail. The gashes were deep, and needed stitches. They had to get Bud to the vet.

Tyler started the ATVs and placed Bud, wrapped in his coat, between his legs on the gas tank. The trip back to the Box W Ranch was fast. Brenda couldn't keep up with Tyler, as her riding skills were not as good as his. Tyler often stopped to wait for her to catch up, so she wouldn't get lost in the dark wilderness.

Once at the Box W Ranch, they spoke briefly with the Waltons, loaded Bud into the front seat of their truck, and headed to town. Betty had called ahead, and the vet was waiting for them when they arrived with the seriously injured dog.

"Bear," the vet said. "Seen it many times before. Nasty critters. They can really work hardship on a dog."

The vet carefully stitched Bud's gaping wounds, then gave him an injection of antibiotics.

"There, that should fix him up. I'll give you some antiseptic salve to keep infection out of the wound. Apply it daily, to keep the wound moist. I'll also give you a supply of the antibiotics in tablet form, just in case it looks like infection may be setting in."

The vet cleaned up the area surrounding the wounds with antiseptic and tenderly rubbed Bud's neck until he felt the animal had settled down and was ready to go home.

The vet explained that infection is a severe threat from bear-inflicted wounds, due partly to the bear's poor hygiene. A bear, for some reason, will lie down and roll in anything foul-smelling. The worse it smells, the better the bear likes it. When encountering a bear in the wild, one can usually smell them before they are seen. Bears in the wild are rank-smelling and nasty.

Brenda was afraid. The mere thought that the bear had been so close to them without their knowledge was enough to cause her genuine concern. Tyler assured Brenda that he would teach her how to fire the guns when they arrived back at the cabin. After seeing what one swat from a bear claw can do to a dog, Brenda was thoroughly convinced that she needed to know how to use a gun.

Bud rested for the next few days. By the evening of the fourth day, he was eating a little and drinking some water. He was able to move, though he was still impaired. Tyler was confident they would be able to make the trip back to the cabin the following day.

The trio arrived at the camp at mid-morning the next day. There was no evidence that any visitors had been around the cabin during their absence. Tyler's first priority was to set up a target and teach Brenda how to load and fire the rifle. Brenda was quick to acquire the skills, and was soon able to fire the gun accurately. Tyler was confident that she was capable of shooting something life-threatening if the need arose. The rifle was a 30.06 caliber, and one properly placed round would send a bear to meet its maker with no problem.

Tyler returned to his work. The next project was to cut a hole in the back wall of the cabin where the fireplace would be built. Unlike a fireplace in a city home, the entire firebox had to be built on the outside of the cabin on the ground, constructed on stones. The stones would be placed in such a way as to form an opening for the fire. The opening cut in the cabin wall would allow the heat to travel from the stone-constructed box and warm the inside of the cabin. Next, a one-foot-square flue built of wood would be constructed, running upward from the fireplace to the top of the roof. Stones would be cemented around the wooden form to make the chimney. The chimney would be attached to the top of the firebox and would extend to the top of the cabin. With the cylinder of stone cemented around the wood, the wooden box would be removed from the opening in the top, leaving a nicely formed rock chimney.

It sounded easy to Tyler, but he struggled to get the chimney to look nice. It took some time, as each cemented layer of stone had to dry and set before he could add the next layer. Tyler spent several days getting it just right before he could accept his job as adequate. The top opening of the chimney was covered with a flat rock. This rock was supported at the corners with small stones that were cemented in place to keep the rain and snow out of the chimney, while still allowing the smoke to escape.

Tyler then proceeded to erect the interior walls of the cabin. The plan that he had drawn called for a bedroom on the back wall of the cabin, next to the fireplace. The bedroom walls would be constructed of two-by-twelve planks purchased in town. In the winter, the fire would warm the rocks of the fireplace and provide heat for the bedroom. The bedroom would be the only closed-off room in the cabin.

The inside bedroom wall would be the back wall of the kitchen, which would be in the front of the cabin. The fireplace would be at the end of the long, L-shaped living room that met the kitchen, which was equipped with a large cookstove that Tyler had purchased. The stove had two large tanks that would be used to heat water. The stovepipe ran from the top of the stove through the roof, allowing the smoke to escape. The stove would provide enough warmth to adequately heat the kitchen area and the front portion of the cabin. Fuel for both the fireplace and the cookstove appeared to be in abundance—they were surrounded by it.

Bud was healing and was starting to snoop around the cabin. He had finally learned to bark, which would be helpful if the bear decided to return. In fact, Bud found several things to bark about during the day, and often at night. Brenda got scared whenever Bud barked, confident that the bear had returned.

The ice was gone from the lake now, and Tyler was happy to find that it contained an ample supply of fish. Brenda and Tyler spent many evenings down at the lake fishing for trout. The fish were excellent eating. The lake water was fresh and ice-cold. There was no contamination in this lake. Most prevalent in the lake were the native cutthroat, and Mackinaw, commonly called "lake trout." Occasionally, a species called "brook trout" or "brookies" could be caught at the outlet of the lake, in the shallow water. Tyler enjoyed catching the fish in the lake. They were scrappy and full of fight. Tyler had mastered the art of fly-fishing, and it was now one of his favorite pastimes.

Brenda and Tyler were anxious to move into the cabin, which was ready for occupancy. The cots were moved into the bedroom and placed neatly along the walls. They were ready to sleep for the first time in their new home.

The Coleman lanterns were brought into the cabin to provide lighting. Brenda and Tyler could now read before retiring to the bedroom. Brenda felt much safer in the cabin and slept well that night, despite Bud's occasional barking. Bud seemed a little nervous in the cabin, and spent most of the night pacing the floor. He had learned to enjoy the outdoors, and preferred the freedom of being outside. It would take a while for him to become used to being a house dog again.

Brenda and Tyler were awakened early the next morning by a loud clap of thunder. Lightning was cracking all around the lake, and Brenda was happy they were safe inside the cabin. The clouds turned loose with torrents of water. Brenda felt warm and snug in the sleeping bag. Listening to the soothing rhythm of the falling rain, she fell back into a deep slumber. It was great to know they were warm, dry, and safe.

Brenda was startled when she heard someone knocking at the cabin door. Tyler, who had gotten up earlier, was surprised to find Betty and Tom Walton standing outside. The couple had ridden their horses up for a visit. They had started before the storm, and were well past the point of returning when the rain came. They were cold and soaked to the bone. Tyler welcomed them inside and put a pot of coffee on. Brenda pulled on her Levi's and a sweatshirt, ran a brush through her hair, and went to greet their guests.

Betty and Tom examined the cabin in great detail and were quite impressed with Tyler's construction. They studied his work closely, marveling at his ingenuity and craftsmanship.

Sipping the hot coffee and huddling around the warm cook-stove, Tom asked about Bud. Tyler whistled for Bud to come, then leaned over to point out the scars, which were just about healed. Tom patted Bud on the head and began to share a story that he had picked up from a forest ranger the previous day. Apparently, a black bear had been spotted dragging down lambs from a band of sheep that were being summer grazed on BLM acreage above Eagle Lake. The sheep herder who had seen the bear shot it, but was unable to track it down. The herder found blood, but the wounded bear wasn't found.

Tom warned Brenda and Tyler that the wounded bear would likely become aggressive. He advised them to be on the lookout for the bear. If they saw it, it would be in their best interest to kill it. Tyler said he would shoot the bear, given the opportunity, but he had no idea which part of the bear's body he should aim for.

Tom took his hand; he placed it on his stomach, above his pants pocket, and moved it up to his shoulder along his side. "Anywhere in this area would do the job," Tom responded. "One good hit any-where in this area will finish the animal off. Heart and lung shot is what you want. Aim behind the front shoulder."

Tyler studied Tom's face, and could tell from his expression that he had a good idea what he was talking about. Tyler had already made the decision that he would shoot the bear if he got the chance. He would carry his loaded rifle with him when leaving the cabin area, and would also keep it handy around the cabin.

After a lengthy visit, the Waltons, warm, dry, and full of coffee, were ready to head back to the ranch. Before they departed, Brenda invited them back for a wilderness cookout. They would have to bring the steaks.

With more work, the cabin started to seem like a home at last. Brenda was making a list of materials she would buy on her next trip to town, to properly adorn the cabin's interior and complete the feeling of being a home.

The next morning, Tyler started building a porch onto the front of the cabin. His plans called for it to extend a few feet out from the cabin wall. The porch would be closed across the front and on one end. This would provide a dry place for wood storage, as well as a break from the wind on chilly days. Building the porch turned out to be a bigger project than Tyler had expected. He finished the roof of the porch as he had the cabin roof, and sided it with logs that matched the logs used on the cabin. It was a nice addition, and would be very practical.

The last major project on Tyler's agenda was to build a storage shed outside the kitchen door, close to the cabin. Tyler wanted it completed before winter. Building the shed would be a rather large project. It had to be large enough to store the ATVs in the winter and the snowmobiles in the summer. Tyler's idea was to build the roof so it hung over on one side, so they could park the ATVs or snowmobiles outside but keep them protected from rain or snow. He decided to work on this over the course of the summer, as it was now time to relax and enjoy their home.

Chapter
Twenty

With the construction nearly completed, Tyler and Brenda were taking more time to enjoy and explore their new environment. Day trips were taken on the ATVs, with Bud riding in a small box on the rear of Tyler's machine. The rifle had also become standard equipment on their outings, strapped securely across the handlebars of Tyler's ATV. Slow, enjoyable rides were taken to areas as far as three or four miles from the cabin. The wildflowers, the wildlife, and the scenery were breathtaking. One of Brenda's favorite spots was near the base of a tree-covered mountain where the water spilled down a rocky slope, forming a beautiful waterfall. Brenda and Tyler sat for hours, basking in the sun and enjoying each other's company and the beautiful landscape.

Times like this made Brenda feel the entire wilderness adventure was worthwhile. Tyler loved to paint, and captured the beautiful view of the waterfall on canvas. Brenda loved the painting and carefully placed it on the wall of the cabin next to the fireplace. The wilderness couple's love for one another had grown to a point of truly dedicated unity. Marriage often crossed Brenda's mind, but marriage would not make their undying love for one another any stronger.

Another spot near the cabin that Brenda had learned to love was what came to be known as "the bathing pool." The pool was situated about one hundred yards above one of the stakes marking Tyler's property line, directly below a large, granite boulder which sat on the edge of the beautiful lake. The small pool was fed by a warm spring that flowed from under the boulder, and had a clean, sandy bottom. The water was very warm. It was a perfect place to bathe and cleanse the soul. Tyler had discovered the hot spring while wading in the lake, fly-fishing one morning. The pool was crystal clear, nearly three feet deep, and the warm temperature would keep it from freezing in the winter. It would be a natural place for animals to drink during the long, cold winter. Tyler and Brenda often built a nice fire and lounged around in the warm pool in the evenings. Brenda loved this place. She fondly referred to it as their "little warm love-pool."

Soon the cabin was completed, and it was wonderfully comfortable. Tyler fashioned the interior with furniture built from natural logs, including a dining table with four chairs. He added two chairs that sat in front of the fireplace before a small, low table. Tyler hung the timber he had used to fight off the moose over the hand-built fireplace. He would not part with that. Shelves were built against the wall for book storage, and kitchen cabinets were constructed to complete the kitchen.

Brenda planned to purchase pillows for the chairs and a bolt of material to be used for curtains. A braided rug for the floor would also be a nice touch. A bed frame was built, and Tyler planned to buy a mattress on the next trip to town. However, he must first figure out a way to get the mattress back to the cabin. His idea was to tie it on the trailer and pull it with the ATV. This later proved to be a workable idea.

While returning one evening from one of the frequent outings that Brenda and Tyler enjoyed, Bud tangled with another porcupine. Tyler had spotted the prickly animal while riding through a small aspen grove at about the same time as Bud. In a flash, Bud had left the box on the rear of the ATV and attacked the porcupine. Biting and snarling, Bud tried desperately to get his teeth into the small animal. The outcome of Bud's attack was mournfully predictable. Tyler stopped, quickly dismounted the ATV, and rushed over to grab him. It was too late. Bud's mouth and face were already full of the porcupine's sharp quills. Fortunately for Bud, none of the quills had penetrated his eyes. Tyler was holding Bud in his arms when Brenda arrived at his side.

Tyler knew what must be done. The thought of the merciless task facing him made him feel sick to his stomach. Brenda was in tears, sympathetically feeling the pain Bud was experiencing. Tyler walked to his ATV and removed the pliers from the toolbox. Bud didn't like the quill removal any better this time that he had the first.

After the quills were removed, Bud was placed on Tyler's lap for the trip back to the cabin. Tyler carefully steered his vehicle down the path. It was getting dark, and travel was slow and tedious. At last, the dark outline of the cabin came into view. Once inside, the lanterns were lit and Tyler began to examine Bud more closely. Bud's face was a terrible, bloody mess.

Tyler cleaned Bud's wounds with disinfectant. Bud bit at Tyler's hand with each swipe of the solution-soaked cloth. It was dreadfully difficult for Brenda to watch Tyler inflicting pain on Bud with the stinging solution. Finally, Tyler was satisfied that he had done all he could do. He wrapped an antibiotic tablet in a piece of wadded-up bread and forced it down Bud's throat. Tyler had saved the leftover tablets from Bud's confrontation with the bear.

Time was the only thing that would make Bud feel better now. Tyler carried him over and laid him down on a blanket that Brenda had folded and placed on the floor.

Tyler gently patted Bud on the back and said, "Old buddy, will you ever learn to leave those prickly little critters alone? If you would, we wouldn't have to do this to you. I know you hate it. So do I."

Bud lay there breathing hard with his eyes half closed, again in severe pain. Nonetheless, he enjoyed the tender affection that he was getting.

Tyler turned to Brenda and said, "I guess the vet was right. He'll never learn to leave them alone."

The healing process was much slower this time. Bud had taken several more of the quills on this encounter than he had the first time. Several days passed before Bud began to act as though he was going to be his normal self again. Bud only left the cabin to relieve himself. Eating, drinking, and short trips outside were his only activities for the next few days.

At last, Bud began to move gingerly about the cabin and clawed at the door to go outside. Tyler and Brenda stayed around the cabin to keep him company, as he got really upset when they tried to leave without him. Tyler painted and Brenda cut and sewed the curtains that would adorn the windows. Tyler hung a few of his artistic creations on the walls of the cabin, which was now taking on a warm, homey feeling. Tyler's artwork was exceptional, and Brenda was confident it could be sold, should Tyler get the urge to sell it.

Even with the hard work and hardships of living in the wilderness, Brenda and Tyler loved every minute of it. Tyler often thought of the life they had left in Chicago, and was happy with the decision he had made. Brenda's mind also wandered back to the big city from time to time. She, too, was happy to be in the cozy little cabin with the man she loved. Tyler was truly a part of her life, and she wanted to be with him forever.

Chapter

Twenty-one

Summer was nearly gone, and the wilderness trio was becoming quite comfortable in the cabin. The storage shed had been completed, and a lot of time was spent enjoying the last few days of summer. Bud was healed now, and life was back to normal.

Early one evening, Bud ran up to the front porch of the cabin, barking and clawing at the front door and begging frantically to be let in. Brenda opened the door with a quick, forceful jerk. Bud squeezed through when the opening was barely wide enough for his body.

"What's the matter, Bud?" Brenda asked. "What's got you excited, big guy?"

Bud had circled the cabin and returned to the half-opened door, growling and barking. The hair on his back was standing straight up, and his tail was tucked tightly between his legs.

Then, Brenda saw the subject of Bud's alarm.

Outside the open door, facing her, was her worst nightmare. The bear was huge. Breathless and gasping for air, Brenda quickly closed the door and slid the bolt closed. She was speechless. Finally, her trembling voice was able to respond to her panic-stricken desire.

"B-b-b-bear!" she shouted.

Tyler jumped from the chair where he had been dozing, startled and confused. He responded as if he had rehearsed the scene a hundred times before. He grabbed the rifle, slid open the bolt, and placed a live round of ammunition in the firing chamber. Cautiously, he crept to the kitchen window and parted the curtain with the index finger of his left hand. Peering out, he gasped, then tried to swallow the huge lump in his throat. The black bear was steadily approaching the entrance to the porch with its nose in the air, sniffing wildly, its huge head turning to explore the surroundings.

Tyler was overtaken with fear. He stared intently, frozen stiff. Brenda grabbed Bud and struggled to maintain her sanity as the sound of the bear sniffing loudly outside the cabin door filled the air. Bud whimpered softly in her arms, anxious to get involved.

Thoughts of what to do raced through Tyler's mind. He continued to study the huge animal through the window as it moved around the porch, curiously sniffing and smelling everything. It turned to smell the small pile of trash Brenda had put in a bucket for disposal, and Tyler saw blood oozing down its front shoulder, down to just above its right leg. The bear's wound was swollen and festered. This must be the animal Tom had mentioned a few days ago.

The inquisitive bear tipped over the bucket and rooted through its contents, recklessly searching for something to eat. After nosing through the trash for what seemed like an eternity, the bear slowly moved from the porch, away from Tyler's view. Tyler leaned back to see if he could spot the intruder through the other window. Carefully, trying not to make a sound, Tyler changed position, hoping to see where the bear had gone.

The bear moved around outside the cabin, sniffing and pawing the ground every few feet. When it reached the storage shed, the animal reared up on its hind legs and placed its front feet on the door, as if it knew it must be shoved to be opened. The bear shook the door violently, then let out a growl that could be heard across the lake. Then, the huge animal lowered its body down on all four feet and meandered in a carefree fashion down toward the lake.

With the bear in retreat, Tyler found himself utterly confused about what to do. Should he sneak out and take a shot at the bear, perhaps wounding it again? This could cause the animal to become more aggressive and cause more trouble for the three of them. Scared and wild with fear, his sincerest desire was to kill the uninvited intruder. What would the bear do if Tyler missed with his bullet? He must find out.

Cautiously, Tyler slid the bolt on the cabin door and opened it as quietly as he could, then crept to the end of the porch. He moved his head forward, his eyes searching madly. The bear had made it to the lake, and had lowered its head to drink. This was his chance. He steadied the rifle against the door opening, and placed the cross hairs in the scope on his target. His thumb slid the rifle's safety to the "off" position. The gun was ready to fire.

Just as Tyler was starting to apply pressure to the trigger with his index finger, his eye picked up movement to the far left of his intended target. It was another bear. Tyler's heart pounded rapidly in his chest. He froze. Slowly, he removed his finger from the trigger and slid the safety back to the "on" position with his thumb. He backed into the doorway of the cabin and closed the door quietly. He slid the door closed, and sat the butt of the gun on the floor.

Placing his right index finger over his lips, he whispered, "There are two bears out there." Tyler saw that Brenda had placed the palm of one hand over her mouth to keep from screaming, while still clutching Bud with the other hand. She was about to lose it.

Together, the couple watched the two bears through the cabin window. The animals meandered slowly down the lake and disappeared into the willow brush about two hundred yards down the beach. They were gone at last, and Brenda took her first deep breath in several minutes. She was fighting to maintain control. She couldn't handle any more of this bear business.

Tyler needed a drink, and he needed it bad. He didn't bother to pour the whiskey into a glass. He just put the bottle to his lips and pulled about three quick bubbles of the liquid into his trembling mouth. The drink quickly found its way to his stomach, and a warm, tingly feeling saturated his tense body.

It was over an hour before Tyler and Brenda could talk freely or relax. Nobody left the cabin that night, and sleep was damn scarce.

Tyler rose at dawn the next morning and carefully scanned the immediate area around the cabin from each window before opening the door to go outside. He proceeded with caution, looking for any evidence that the bears were still present. Tyler carried the rifle in his hands, holding the weapon across his chest, ready to aim and fire if the bears were seen. There was no evidence that the bears had returned to the cabin during the night. Tyler slowly walked down to the lake. After studying the tracks in the sand, he dropped the gun to his side and returned to the cabin, confident that the uninvited intruders were gone.

Tyler poured a cup of coffee and sat down at the table to collect his thoughts. What should he do now? Should he continue his search and try to find the bear? Or should he leave well enough alone, and let the bears do what they may? He gazed at his half-empty coffee mug, searching his busy mind for the most logical approach to his dilemma. He finally made up his mind. He must go search for the wounded bear and its companion and attempt to kill them.

Brenda had gotten dressed, and she walked out of the bedroom with a look of concern on her face. "Tyler, I can't stand this. We can't go on like this. I won't sleep until I know the bear is gone—for good. I'm scared, Tyler, really scared."

Tyler reached for Brenda's hand and pulled her over to him, setting her on his lap. "I know, Brenda; I too am concerned. I can't relax, knowing that the bear could show up at any moment. I have to kill those bastards—especially the wounded one."

Brenda was starting to sob now. "What did we do to that damn bear? Why doesn't he leave us alone?"

Tyler wiped away the tear that was creeping down Brenda's pretty face. "I'll take the gun and see if I can find the bear. If I can find him, I'll solve our problem, once and for all."

Tyler placed several rounds of ammunition in the large pocket of his coat, then picked up the rifle and put four rounds in the magazine. He closed the bolt carefully, making certain a live round didn't enter the barrel. Before leaving, Tyler took the pistol from the bedroom and placed it on the table.

"This is loaded, so be careful. It's ready to fire if you need it."

He leaned over and gave Brenda a kiss on the forehead. Brenda, with tear-filled eyes, looked up at him and said, "Please be careful, Tyler. Don't be gone long. Please."

Tyler patted her on the head and said, "Don't worry, Brenda, I won't be far. I'll keep the cabin in sight. If you need me, give a yell. I'll be close enough to hear you."

Tyler reached for the door, turning to look at Brenda. "Make sure you bolt the door after I leave."

Before he left the porch, Tyler heard the bolt slide into place. He walked down to the lake, found the bear tracks in the loose sand, and began to follow them down to where they disappeared into the cover of the brush. Slowly and carefully, Tyler worked his way through the heavy brush, scanning every inch for any sign of the bears. He followed the shoreline of the lake, working his way through the brush. Occasionally he turned to check the cabin, where he saw Brenda nervously peering out the larger window.

After a few minutes of searching, Tyler came upon a small clearing covered with long, stiff grass. The grass was mashed flat along one edge of the clearing, as if something had been laying there recently. After close examination of the area, Tyler was able to find what appeared to be dried blood. It was apparent that the animal had probably rested here most of the night. Tyler felt goose bumps rise on the back of his neck at the thought. He stood there, motionless, thinking about the bear having been that close. The only instinct he had was to get away. However, he must continue his search.

Tyler's rapidly searching eyes caught bare ground through the brush up on the side of a small hill which overlooked his position. As quickly as possible, he worked his way up the hill to the clearing. Once there, he turned to scan the area between himself and the lake. He saw nothing, but his eyes continued to search. Suddenly, Tyler caught a black flash moving through the brush about two hundred yards down the lake. He froze, holding his breath, his heart pounding wildly. The huge bear was cautiously ambling away with his head held high, looking back in Tyler's direction. Tyler grabbed the bolt of the rifle and pulled it back quickly, then pushed it forward, placing a live round in the barrel. The rifle was ready to fire. Tyler studied the area, waiting, holding his breath, and his pounding heart seemed as if it would explode. He stood, frozen like a statue, searching for another glimpse of the bear. Finally, the majestic beast came back into view, slowly working its way up the other side of the hill.

Now was his chance. Tyler raised the rifle and put the cross hairs of the scope right over the shoulder of the bear, just as Tom had instructed. The bear continued to walk slowly, sniffing the air for danger as it moved. After a moment, the animal stopped.

Tyler slowly applied pressure to the rifle's trigger. The large gun bucked, smashing into Tyler's shoulder like the kick of a mule. The blast knocked Tyler off balance, making him slightly dizzy and disoriented. The percussion was deafening. Gathering his senses, Tyler frantically searched the area for the bear. He could see nothing.

Just then, Tyler sighted the beast topping the hill on a dead run. Tyler had missed. Disheartened and discouraged, he slowly lowered the rifle to his side and dropped his head.

Damn, he thought. How the hell could I have missed him? The bear was gone now, and he had to return to the cabin and tell Brenda about his failure. The fear would continue.

He walked back to the cabin, cursing to himself along the way. He was on the beach when Brenda opened the door and ran to the edge of the porch, with Bud close by her side.

"What happened, Tyler? Did you get him?"

"No, I missed," he responded. "I can't believe it. The last I saw of that son of a bitch, he was headed up over the hill. He won't be back for a while. I put some wheels on him."

Tyler had suffered from the inevitable "buck fever" that most new hunters experience. He had waited for a long time to get that shot. He felt genuinely disappointed that he had missed the bear. He was left only with the hope that he would do better the next time.

Chapter
Twenty-two

It was late in the fall, and the beautiful aspen leaves were starting to don their radiant autumn colors. Tyler spent countless hours behind his easel on a hillside, capturing the serene beauty of the season on canvas. Brenda and Bud explored the area, careful to stay within range of Tyler.

The fall was beautiful. Deer and elk showed their heavy, plush coats, preparing themselves for the long winter ahead. Brenda often sat and listened to the bugling elk in the distance. The bugling, a high-pitched, whistling sound, notified the cows of the bull's presence, and also served to warn other bulls in the area of his dominance. The bull would fight to maintain this dominance as the mating season approached. Upon hearing the bull, others in the area would return the bugle, as if to challenge. The bulls would fight for hours. The clashing of their heavy antlers could be heard over great distances. Eventually one of the bulls would be declared the victor, and the challengers would travel on to seek other bulls for the fight. The fighting and bugling would continue until the breeding season was over.

Elk have another characteristic that is not commonly known. Every elk, whether a cow or a bull, has two solid ivory teeth in its jaw. Once the elk is killed, the ivory teeth, molars, can be removed. They are often carried in the hunter's pocket or used to make attractive and unusual rings, earrings, or key chains.

The turning leaves signaled the coming of the long, hard winter. The evenings were becoming cooler, and during the day a light jacket or sweater was welcomed. Tyler had loaded the porch with wood, and would soon stockpile a large amount around the cabin. Tyler and Brenda looked forward to the coming winter with a little apprehension, not knowing what to expect or how they would handle the countless hours of isolation. It would be a challenge.

The hunting season had started, and the deer and elk could often be seen moving about the area in search of protection from the hunters. Just before dark one evening, the hair on Bud's back rose and he began to bark at the cabin door. Tyler, who had been relaxing in a chair in front of the fireplace, jumped up and grabbed the gun before going to see what had upset Bud. Could the bear be back? Tyler crept over to the window and parted the curtain for a look outside. He could see the outline of what appeared to be a human coming up to the cabin from the lake. He opened the door and walked out on the porch. The silence of the late fall evening was broken by the words of the stranger.

"Hi there," the stranger said. "I'm lost. I saw your lights. May I come in?"

Tyler examined the stranger momentarily before responding, "Sure, come in."

The stranger stepped up on the porch and extended his right hand. "I'm Monte Pilcher. My friends and I have a camp somewhere around here. We're up here hunting."

Tyler reached out and shook his hand. "Tyler's my name. This is Brenda, and this little critter is Bud."

The lost hunter entered the cabin, pulled his cap from his head, and held it in his hand. "Nice to meet you, Tyler. You too, Brenda. I've been hunting up on the rim above the head of the lake. I lost my bearings and I'm looking for our camp. I'm not quite sure where it is."

Tyler walked over and sat the rifle in the corner. "Got any idea which direction it is from here?" he asked.

"Not a clue," the hunter responded. "Walked up on the rim at daybreak. Seems like it should be on further down that direction." He pointed across the lake from the cabin.

"Can I pour you a cup of coffee?" Tyler asked.

"That would be great," the hunter responded. He unbuttoned the top button of his jacket before asking, "Do you know a rancher in these parts by the name of Lee?"

Tyler poured a hot cup of coffee and handed it to the visitor. "Lee Thomas. I know him. You hunting with Lee?"

"Yes, that's it, Lee Thomas," the hunter said, sipping the coffee. "There are four of us camped up on a rim due east of the Rocking R Ranch."

"Have a seat," Tyler offered.

The man sat down and let out a large groan, implying that he was tired. "Thanks for the hospitality. I really appreciate the coffee," he said.

Tyler and Monte visited until Monte placed the empty mug on the table. Tyler retrieved his map and spread it on the table to show Monte where he was. After studying the map for a while, the hunter pointed to one spot and said, "I think our camp is in this area."

Tyler looked at the map and replied, "I know the area. It must be about three miles from here."

Monte looked again at the map before saying, "How the hell did I get that far from our camp?"

"It's easy," Tyler said. "It's not hard to get lost in the woods if you don't pay attention."

After a bit more conversation, Tyler offered to give Monte a ride back to his camp on the ATV. Although Monte seemed reluctant to accept, Tyler could tell he was relieved to have a ride. Darkness was already upon them.

Tyler told Brenda he'd be back in about an hour. He grabbed the rifle and a flashlight, and left to return the lost hunter. He secured the rifle to the handlebars of the vehicle and told Monte the best way to sit on the rear rack. Rider in place, the two headed out to find the lost hunter's camp.

Tyler steered the ATV down the lake, trying to find a trail that headed up the rise to its other side. He picked his way through the brush and proceeded up the mountain directly across from the cabin, then pointed the ATV south. Travel was tough in the dark, and with the added weight of the passenger Tyler was forced to pick his way through the rocks and trees slowly. At last, Tyler steered the ATV into a small clearing on a bluff which overlooked the valley leading down to the Rocking R Ranch. He immediately spotted a campfire, which undoubtedly belonged to the hunting party. Working his way down the small mountain to the bottom, he drove the ATV into the camp to deliver his passenger, whose companions were happy and relieved to see their friend.

Monte introduced Tyler and praised him for his gracious hospitality. Tyler visited with the hunters for a few minutes before commenting that he must get back to the cabin. He told them of the wounded bear in the area, and warned them to be extremely careful where they placed their food at night. The hunters listened with keen concern, and advised Tyler that they would take extra precautions. Monte thanked Tyler again for the ride, and Tyler began his trip back to the cabin.

Tyler felt a cold, empty feeling as he rode up the mountain to the ridge that led back in the direction of the cabin. It was totally dark now, and the dim lights of the ATV made traveling quite hazardous. Tyler was forced to slowly pick his way through the rocks and trees.

Reaching the point on the ridge where he would start his descent to the lake, Tyler suddenly lost control of the ATV. It swerved hard to the left, and the right front wheel struck a large boulder, jerking the vehicle back to the right. The momentum of the unexpected turn caused the ATV to raise up on two wheels. It happened so fast that Tyler was unable to keep the vehicle upright. It rolled over to the left, crushing Tyler beneath it as it rolled down the mountainside. The vehicle flipped several times before coming to rest on its top, leaving Tyler's body in a heap several feet back up the slope. The weight of the vehicle had landed directly on Tyler's knee during the ordeal.

Tyler lay motionless, attempting to collect his wits before assessing the damage. His knee was numb and felt about the size of a large ham. He slowly straightened his leg and raised his body to a sitting position. Though shaken and scared, he was able to stand. He worked his way down to the ATV and leaned against it, gasping to catch his breath.

His knee was sore and throbbing as he hobbled around the ATV, trying to figure out a way to get the vehicle upright. After much time and thought he was able to grab the vehicle from the downhill side and pull it toward himself to roll it upright. He leaned against the seat and rested. The vehicle's engine had quit running in the accident, and Tyler turned the ignition switch to the "off" position. Several minutes passed before he was able to crawl up on the seat. Tyler noticed that the gas tank had leaked fuel while the vehicle was upside down. He reached for the ignition key and turned it. The engine fired immediately, and the ATV seemed to run fine.

Tyler then remembered the rifle that he had strapped to the handlebars. It had apparently come loose in the accident and was missing. He reached for the flashlight and hobbled back up the hill. He found the rifle stuck barrel-down in the dirt, planted there by the weight of the vehicle when it rolled over. Tyler pulled it from the dirt and brushed it off with his hand. Hobbling back to the ATV, he replaced the rifle in its original position and crawled back onto the seat. Slowly, he squeezed the throttle and started down the mountain.

The machine made it to the bottom, directly across the lake from the cabin, before the engine sputtered and quit. Tyler reached for the ignition key and attempted to start the stalled engine. It wouldn't start. Remembering the spilled fuel, he reached for the fuel cap and removed it. The tank was empty. Tyler must now hobble as best as he could for the remaining distance to the cabin.

Flashlight and rifle in hand, Tyler left the ATV and limped through the brush. He remembered telling Brenda that he would be gone for about an hour. Glancing at his watch, he realized he had already been gone an hour and was still an hour away. Brenda will be frantic, he thought to himself.

The trip was painfully slow for Tyler as he navigated through the rocks and brush around the lake to the cabin. He arrived exhausted and in severe pain from the badly swollen knee. The walking had further stressed the damaged knee.

"Brenda, it's me," he called from outside the cabin.

The cabin door opened and Bud ran out, barking wildly, with Brenda close behind.

"What happened, Tyler?" Brenda asked. "Where's the ATV?"

Tyler reached for the open door and hobbled inside the cabin. "I had a little accident," he responded. "Turned it over up on the mountain and spilled all the fuel. Hurt my damn knee in the process." He eased himself into a chair.

"How far did you walk?" Brenda asked.

"Just from the other side of the lake," Tyler answered. "Wouldn't have been bad if I hadn't messed up my knee. I could sure use a drink, if you don't mind."

Brenda retrieved the bourbon from the kitchen shelf and placed it with a glass on the table. Tyler poured about three fingers into the glass, knocked it back, and swallowed. The fluid felt warm inside him, and the pain in his knee became superficially less important.

The next morning, Tyler found walking quite painful. The knee had remained swollen and had turned various shades of blue and purple. Though in pain, Tyler felt thankful that he had managed to come through the accident as well as he had. He wouldn't attempt to get the ATV yet. He would keep his damaged knee propped in the air all day, while Brenda waited on him, hand and foot.

Finally, around noon on the third day, Tyler told Brenda that they should take some gasoline and get the ATV. Brenda drove while Tyler sat in the rear with the gasoline can. Once fueled, the machine started, and Tyler and Brenda rode back to the cabin, mission accomplished.

Chapter
Twenty-three

Several days passed. Tyler hobbled around the cabin with the assistance of a crutch he had fashioned from a willow branch that Brenda had found. Though crude, the crutch served its purpose and was a great help to Tyler. His knee had apparently suffered some ligament damage, and there was no evidence that it would feel much better in the near future.

Tyler spent his days of confinement reading and watching the wildlife that could be seen through the cabin's windows with the binoculars. Deer and elk could often be spotted moving in small herds around the edge of the lake. Occasionally, a large bull moose would come to eat the grass on the other side. The fearless animal would eat and drink for hours before disappearing into the tall brush.

Brenda began putting crackers and nuts out on a large, flat rock beside the cabin. Chipmunks, rabbits, and squirrels came and munched happily. The rabbits were strange-looking, and seemed interested in Tyler and Brenda. They were very shy, and hopped awkwardly around the outside of the cabin. They had the appearance of typical prairie jackrabbits except for their feet, which were huge. With the assistance of a wildlife identification book, Tyler was able to determine that the animals were snowshoe rabbits, and were commonly found in the wilderness of the mountains. The critter acquired its name by the size of its feet, which were disproportionately large to enable it to negotiate the deep snow of winter. The snowshoe rabbit could move around without breaking through the crusted snow, staying on its surface, which made travel much easier and faster. Catching a snowshoe rabbit would be nearly impossible for a fox or coyote once the snow became deep. Another distinctive feature of the snowshoe rabbit was its ability to change colors. In the dead of winter its coat would turn snow white, blending with the surrounding snow—another of its unique survival tools.

The squirrels who visited the feeding area were small and gray. Often, as many as ten of the furry creatures could be seen munching on Brenda's generous food donations. The squirrels would come up to the rock and stuff the food into their mouths until they looked nearly deformed. Stuffed to the limit, they would scamper away to store the food for future use during the long, brutal winter.

The chipmunks were on the same program. Several trips were made during the day to stuff their little pouches with food for storage. Brenda was amazed at how unbelievably tame and unafraid the animals were getting. Sometimes, she could get as close as a few feet away with offerings of food for her little friends. The animals acted as though they wanted to trust their provider, but their inborn fear of humans wouldn't allow them to get too close. They would sit motionless near the rock as Brenda replenished the food supply, waiting to be the first so their little pouches could be stuffed for the trip back to the nest.

Each morning, the rock would be picked clean of food. The animals would play around the area and wait for Brenda to return with more. Brenda was developing quite a group of trusting little friends.

Bud often stood at the window, ears upright, observing the little animals. Occasionally, when allowed to go outside, he would scatter the little creatures, knowing that Brenda would scold him for doing it. Bud could resist anything but temptation.

Among the frequent visitors around the cabin were a doe and her yearling fawn. Brenda placed apples and carrots near the rock for the deer to eat. Brenda and Tyler watched them munch on the fruit, admiring their beauty and cautious mannerisms.

"Tyler, they are so cute and harmless, how could anyone kill one of those little creatures?"

Tyler grinned, gave Brenda a hug, and said, "Most people haven't learned to love them as you and I have, Brenda. Makes you feel as though you own them, and want to protect them from harm. We must learn to enjoy them, but not get attached to them."

Brenda and Tyler knew that the snow of winter was not far away. They needed to make a trip to town to gather their winter supplies while the weather was nice. Tyler, still having problems with his knee, convinced himself that a trip to see the doctor was in order. Brenda spent a lot of time making lists of items needed for warmth, recreation, and survival. The plan was to take both ATVs and trailers, as the supply list had become quite extensive. The thought of the coming winter held a feeling of anxiety for the two mountain people and their dog. It wouldn't be long before snow fell. The temperature was starting to dip below freezing, and the animals had just about finished growing their plush winter coats.

Fall in Wyoming was beautiful. The first hard freeze would send the colorful leaves fluttering to the ground, leaving the limbs bare and drab, as though they were dead. The turning of the leaves at the higher elevations begins in late September and continues down the mountains through most of October. Snow could be expected above the tree line, near ten thousand feet, anytime after the first of September. Brenda had noticed that the higher peaks above the cabin were turning white, signaling the arrival of winter. Herds of game could be seen moving down the mountains to escape the frigid temperatures and snow cover, seeking areas where grass could still be found. The grass had not grown in over a month and was starting to take on the drab, lifeless color of winter dormancy.

Brenda and Tyler decided to leave the cabin the next day for the ride to the Waltons' and on into town. Tyler spent the better part of the day preparing the vehicles and the trailers for the trip. He placed two tarps on the trailers that could be used to cover their loads. Bud was skittish, nervously pacing around the cabin. He knew something was up, and he was worried to death that he wouldn't be a part of it. Before the trio left for town, the cabin was locked and made as secure as possible. Though there was no evidence that the bear had been around, Tyler knew it could show up at any time. The bear could effortlessly tear the door off the cabin if it decided it wanted to get inside, especially if it thought it might find food there.

The travelers were on the trail and headed to the Waltons' ranch before nine o'clock, traveling slowly and taking time to enjoy the beautiful scenery along the way. They arrived shortly after eleven o'clock and were greeted by Betty and Tom, who invited the travelers in for a cup of coffee. While drinking the coffee and visiting, Tyler told Tom of his experience with the bear, and how he had missed when he fired a shot. Tom listened intently to Tyler's story before informing him that there were many hunters bringing back stories of bear sightings. He warned Tyler and Brenda to be careful in their travels and to keep a keen eye out for bears.

"Apparently, the big black beast was still mad about being wounded and is still aggressive," Tom said. "It would really be nice if you could shoot that troublesome bastard, Tyler. Bears get pretty smart, and it's kind of hard to get a shot, sometimes."

After they finished their coffee, Tyler and Brenda left the Waltons' ranch for their home in town, where they showered and rested before finding a restaurant for a welcome, prepared meal.

The house in town was just as neat and orderly as when they had left a few weeks earlier. It was a bit chilly, but Tyler quickly took care of that by building a nice fire. The showers were wonderful and warm, making them feel very lazy. They napped for a bit, but the idea of a nice dinner made climbing from the bed easy. They had nothing in the house to eat, and Bud, too, was hungry.

Their itinerary included a trip to the doctor's office for an examination of Tyler's knee. Tyler was not surprised when the doctor told him that he had a torn ligament, and that surgery was recommended. After a lengthy discussion of the consequences of not having the knee surgically repaired, Tyler decided to wait and see if it would heal on its own. He left the doctor's office with the understanding that if he didn't get the knee repaired, the chances of a full recovery were slim.

It took Tyler and Brenda the better part of two days to get to the bottom of their shopping list. Every item was checked off the list, and the truck was loaded to its capacity. They planned to head back to the cabin first thing the next day.

Tom and Betty helped Tyler and Brenda transfer the materials from the truck to the trailers, securing the loads with the tarps for the return trip to the cabin. It was threatening rain, and Tyler was happy he had remembered to bring the tarps. Tom and Betty said good-bye to their friends, and advised them of their plans to come up in the near future for a visit. Bud was loaded into the box on the rear of Tyler's ATV, and the trip back to the cabin was underway.

Rain was just starting to fall when the travelers arrived back at the cabin. Tyler and Brenda unloaded their purchases and stacked them in a corner. The trip had been tough on Tyler's knee, and he needed to rest.

"We'll leave this stuff here for tonight and get it sorted and put away tomorrow," Tyler said. "My knee is throbbing. I need to get it elevated for a while. Would you pour me a drink?"

"Sure. Mixed or straight?"

"Straight. It'll help to numb the pain a little."

Brenda put the glass on the table and Tyler quickly drained it. "Damn, that was good. Better pour me another."

Tyler nursed his second drink. Soon he was sound asleep, sitting upright in the chair.

Tyler's knee must be hurting him much worse than I had imagined, Brenda thought. Perhaps I should have encouraged him to stay in town and have the knee repaired. Maybe it's just the strain of all the activity from the trip. Perhaps it will be better tomorrow.

Brenda was worried. The last thing she wanted was to be in the wilderness with Tyler immobile and unable to protect her. She gently rubbed Tyler on the shoulder to wake him and helped him to the bedroom. It was a perfect evening to curl up in front of the fireplace and read the new magazines that she had purchased in town. The rain gently peppering the roof of the cabin was a nice accompaniment to the romantic warmth of the fire she had built. It was a soothing, relaxing evening. Brenda was happy to be back inside the cozy cabin, out of the weather. She wished Tyler were well, and that he was sharing the same feelings as she was. Too bad Tyler went to bed, she thought to herself.

Chapter

Twenty-four

The couple awakened to a beautiful sight the next morning. Sometime during the night, the rain had turned to snow and covered their mountain paradise with a six-inch blanket of pure white softness. The sun was shining, and the clouds had disappeared. Brenda and Tyler sipped their steaming coffee as they peered out the cabin windows. They remarked to each other how beautiful the landscape was with its new, clean covering. The entire area had taken on a totally different personality. Even the mirroring lake seemed more colorful, reflecting the white snow and dark blue sky. It was such a peaceful view that they didn't want to leave the cabin, and interrupt the serenity.

"Time to go to work," Tyler said. "We need to gather some wood, just in case."

Brenda looked at Tyler with a puzzled look on her face. "Just in case of what, Tyler?"

"Could be an early winter, and wood will be easier to get now than later. Do you want to help me?"

Brenda pointed to the pile of supplies stacked in the corner and said, "I'll work on this first, then come help you as soon as I'm done."

Tyler responded, "See you outside in a little while. Dress warm, and be sure to wear your gloves."

Tyler opened the cabin door and limped outside. It was apparent that his knee was bothering him. Hobbling to the storage shed, he retrieved the chain saw, ax, and splitting wedge. The snow was not so deep that it prevented him from using the ATV, which still had the trailer attached. Tyler placed the tools on the trailer and slowly mounted the vehicle to begin his chore. It was a short ride to the area where the cutting would be done. Several large pine trees

were down behind the cabin. The trees had been down long enough
to dry out, and would make excellent firewood.

Brenda heard the noisy chain saw start and shuddered to think
of spoiling the beautiful solitude of early winter. She did, however,
understand the importance of having plenty of wood stockpiled.

Tyler was hobbling around cautiously on his painful knee, cutting the wood in eighteen-inch lengths—the perfect fit for the fireplace. He was meticulous, cutting the wood in uniform lengths. This
would make it easy to stack the wood in a neat pile. Tyler had asked
Tom how much wood would be needed to last the winter. His best
estimate was somewhere between six and eight cords, a cord being
a pile four feet wide, four feet high, and eight feet long. Two cords
of cut and stacked wood would be a big day of cutting for a crippled
guy and a petite city girl.

Tyler had cut, hauled, and stacked two trailer loads before
Brenda exited the cabin to help. The wood was stacked close to the
storage shed, near the kitchen door. The shed would provide a nice
windbreak, and the wood would be conveniently accessible from the
kitchen. Brenda and Tyler worked hard, between frequent rest
intervals, for the better part of the day. After about one and a half
cords were cut and stacked, the couple decided that they had cut
enough for one day. Tyler's knee was starting to hurt even more.
Perhaps he had overdone it a little. The snow was now starting to
melt and drip from the cabin roof, warmed by the shining sun.

The rest of the day was spent inside the cabin. Tyler propped
his leg up on a chair near a window where he could observe the
wildlife moving cautiously through the new-fallen snow. Brenda sat
close beside him, watching the skittish deer sniff around the rock
where they were used to finding snacks of apples and vegetables.
Brenda couldn't stand the disappointment on their innocent faces.
They pricked up their ears and gazed toward the cabin as if to say,
"Where is our food?" Brenda went outside to replenish the supply
for them. She returned from her mission only moments before the
animals came back, cautiously moving forward to nibble away at the
treats. They were beautiful, and seemed appreciative of the gifts. It
was nearly sundown before they trotted away into the trees, as if
needing to get home before dark.

The cabin lanterns were lit and the rest of the evening was
spent with Brenda displaying utter dominance over Tyler in cards.
She handily beat him at three hands of gin rummy. Smiling

deviously and rolling her eyes back in her head as she laid her cards down, she announced, "Gin rummy!"

"Again?" Tyler responded. "You are too damn tough for me. Can't we play a game that I can win?"

"How about Old Maid?" Brenda asked.

Tyler smiled and reached for Brenda's hand. He pulled her to him and kissed her gently on the lips. "Don't ever leave me, Brenda," Tyler said. "I love you. I want you with me always."

Brenda melted into Tyler's arms and fought back the tears that were trying desperately to escape from her smiling eyes. She placed her head on his chest and thought, This is the first time he has told me he loves me. She was ecstatic. Brenda had waited nearly two years to hear Tyler say that. The tears were now flowing down her beautiful face, and she couldn't stop them. Her gentle heart and sincere love for Tyler made composure impossible. She sat in Tyler's lap and wept like a baby, painfully happy that Tyler had finally shared his feelings for her. They sat there for nearly an hour in each other's arms before Tyler led Brenda to the bedroom.

The next few days were spent cutting, hauling, and stacking more wood. The weather had warmed and most of the snow had disappeared, but the snow's presence had served as a reminder of the dire necessity of having an ample supply of wood before winter came to stay.

It was Saturday, and Brenda reminded Tyler of the visit planned by the Waltons. Brenda spent the morning cleaning the cabin and preparing for their guests. Dinner would include spaghetti covered with meat sauce and a large dinner salad. Tyler retrieved a nice bottle of red wine from the storage area beneath the cabin, and everything was in order for a relaxing visit and a nice dinner with their friends.

The Waltons arrived on horseback shortly after one o'clock. Betty and Tom had brought a couple of loaves of fresh home-baked bread with them. The couples had a nice visit. The ladies enjoyed a glass of wine while Tom and Tyler sipped whiskey. During their conversation, Tom inquired about the bear. Tyler told him that they had not seen it for quite some time. Tom listened intently, as if his interest in the bear was more than just casual. His questions were directed at Tyler, and a tone of grave concern was in his voice.

"I keep hearing stories that the bear is still around and making quite a nuisance of himself. Seems to be on the prowl, raiding hunting camps regularly. I guess the old bastard hasn't really hurt anyone, but it seems to enjoy making a total wreck of camps while the hunters are gone. You really need to be careful, Tyler," he said.

Tyler took a sip of his bourbon before responding. "Brenda and I have been very cautious. We haven't seen any sign of him for a couple of weeks now."

"He will be back, Tyler, as long as the weather remains good and he isn't forced into hibernation."

Tom went on, talking about the habits of the black bear. "Black bears are very inquisitive. They probably spend more time watching you than you would believe. They have been known to follow humans and closely observe their habits for long periods of time.

"Traditionally, bears won't get too far away from the forest. The trees provide security for them, and they find comfort in their ability to climb trees for safety. Their diets consist mainly of roots, fruits, and other vegetation. Though a black bear can often be observed eating insects, it seldom has a taste for meat."

Tom continued: "However, black bears have been known to eat many kinds of meat, once it has spoiled and rotted. A bear will kill its prey, hide the carcass, and wait for it to rot before eating it. Bears seldom devour fresh meat from a kill.

"The black bear can range in size from a small cub to a three to four-hundred-pound adult. Its color can range from a dark tan to a deep black. The noticeable difference between a black bear and a grizzly is the shape of the face. The black bear has a long, narrow snout, while the grizzly has a pudgy, shorter snout. The grizzly bear also has more of a rounded hump on his front shoulders than the black bear. Though the grizzly is normally much larger, a young grizzly can sometimes resemble a black bear. I've never seen a grizzly in these parts, though," Tom added.

Tyler and Brenda listened carefully as Tom explained the characteristics of the bear and how to respect its territory. They would certainly be happy if they never saw the bear again.

After a few hours of visiting, Brenda and Betty went to the kitchen to prepare the meal. Tom, Tyler, and Bud walked down to the lake for some fresh air. Once they reached the lake, they turned and strolled down the beach a short distance. Tom stopped and stooped down to examine a print in the sand.

"Bear track," Tom said. "Big old rascal. He's been down this beach in the last day or so."

Tyler leaned over to examine the fresh track. "Sure enough," Tyler said. "This is fresh, probably last night."

"I would guess this track was made by a large, mature male," Tom said. "Judging from the size of the track, I would say this guy weighed nearly four hundred pounds." He reached down and placed his open hand across the track. "Nearly eight inches across," he commented.

Tyler compared the size of Tom's hand with that of the bear print. Then, he rose up and placed his hand on Tom's shoulder. "Please, let's keep this from Brenda. She'll worry herself sick if she knows the bear has been around again."

Tom looked Tyler in the eye and said, "I won't tell, Tyler."

Brenda opened the back door of the cabin, and called, "Dinner is ready, guys!" Tyler looked at Tom, winked, and grinned slightly, and they headed up to the cabin for dinner.

The dinner was well received by the guests and enjoyed by all. The wine was excellent—so good, in fact, that Tyler fetched and opened another bottle. The table was cleared, and the two couples settled around the dinner table for a few hands of cards and some coffee. It was a nice, relaxed afternoon.

Soon it came time for the Waltons to head home. Thanking Brenda and Tyler for the dinner, they climbed up on their horses and headed back to the ranch. It was late afternoon, but there was plenty of time for them to make it home before dark.

With their stomachs full of dinner and wine, Brenda and Tyler spent the evening relaxing and reading, but Tyler was troubled that Tom had spotted fresh bear tracks.

I must kill that bear, Tyler thought. The bear's unwelcome intrusion into their private lives and happiness had convinced Tyler that their little world was too small for its presence.

Tyler gazed into the fire with a look of intensity. He thought to himself, I will get that bastard; he can't ruin our lives and contentment. It may take some time, and a lot of ingenuity, but I will get him.

The determination driving Tyler was a combination of bravery and fear. He stood and walked over to the window, studying the underbrush and trees in the general direction of the lake. "I think I'll take the rifle and stroll down around the lake. Want to come with me?" he asked Brenda.

She raised her eyes from the book she was reading and looked at Tyler. "No, I think I'll just stay in the cabin, unless you especially want me to come."

Tyler picked up the rifle and glanced over at Brenda. He replied, "No, you stay. I won't be long. I just want to get some fresh air and exercise my knee a little. See you in a few minutes. Come on, Bud, let's go."

Tyler pulled the cabin door closed behind him and walked down the path toward the lake. He limped noticeably for the first few steps until his knee limbered a little. The evening air was cool, and a gentle breeze drove it through his shirt, chilling his body. Bud ran wildly toward the lake and circled through the short bushes, stopping a couple of times to relieve himself. Tyler worked his way down to the sand and headed toward the head of the lake. He searched the ground carefully to see if he could find more tracks.

As he reached the edge of the sandy beach where the under-brush took over, he found more telltale signs. On the ground in the grass next to the lake were bear scats—bear droppings. Though an experienced biologist could quickly determine from scats what the bear has been eating, Tyler couldn't be sure. There appeared to be some evidence of hair or fur in the scats, which caused goose bumps to rise on the back of his neck.

Tyler and Bud continued to stroll down the edge of the lake for a few hundred yards before Tyler decided they should get back to the cabin. "Come on, Bud, let's go back." Bud darted out of the nearby brush to walk beside Tyler.

Inside the cabin, Tyler placed the rifle in the corner of the kitchen and checked the wood supply. Noticing that the wood box was nearly empty, he walked out the kitchen door to the neatly stacked woodpile and grabbed an arm load. After placing the wood in the wood box he walked over to Brenda, who was still reading her book.

"Brenda, I don't want to alarm you, but I feel you should know that I found evidence that the bear has been around here again."

Brenda placed the open book in her lap and looked up at Tyler. "How can you tell—did you see it?"

"No, just a fresh sign," Tyler said. "Down by the lake—tracks and droppings. Nothing to get too alarmed about, but be careful when you go outdoors. It may still be around here."

Brenda stared at Tyler for several moments before saying, "Damn it, Tyler, I want you to get rid of that damn thing. Can't you hunt it down and kill it?"

Tyler sat down beside Brenda and said, "Yes, I can. I plan to do my best to get that creature out of our lives forever."

"How?"

"Well, I'm not sure if I should try to bait it, or just wait for it to come snooping around again. I think I'll leave some fresh garbage out in front of the cabin, and rig up a device that will alert us of its presence—a string or cord attached to something inside the cabin that will signal us. What do you think?"

"We have to try something, Tyler. I can't go on like this."

"I'll rig up something in the morning," Tyler said. "I have an idea that might work."

Tyler and Brenda spent the rest of the evening indoors and retired early. Brenda slept well, but Tyler was restless. His mind was a beehive of activity, searching for a way to devise an alarm to warn them of the bear's presence.

Tyler got up early the next morning. He had an idea, and was working diligently to perfect it. Though it was a little elementary and quite crude, he thought his idea might work.

His plan was to tie a piece of cord to a tree and stretch it close to the ground, up to and under the cabin door. The cord would be attached to an eating utensil placed inside a large pan. If an animal approached the area where he planned to place the garbage, it would hit the cord, causing the utensil to clatter against the pan. The noise would surely wake them. He could then sneak out of the cabin and shoot the bear. Tyler was confident that his idea would work.

The alarm was baited and set just as darkness came that evening. The intensity with which Tyler pursued his project caused Brenda some concern. It was almost as if Tyler knew something that he wasn't sharing with her. Tyler placed the loaded rifle near the door, beside a five-cell flashlight. Bud, too, was edgy, as if he knew something was up. Bud nervously paced the floor, stopping periodically to sniff the large pan which was to be the signaling device. The pan had to be moved twice, as Bud kept hitting the cord and sounding the alarm system that Tyler had devised. There was no doubt that the invention would wake them if an animal should run into the cord.

Brenda and Tyler doused the lanterns and retired shortly after ten o'clock. The silence was thick. Tyler lay in bed, waiting for the alarm to sound, before falling asleep.

Shortly after midnight, the utensil in the pan clattered, likely signaling the arrival of a garbage guest. Tyler woke quickly and jumped from the bed. As quietly as he could, he crept out the bedroom door and tiptoed to the kitchen window. Straining his eyes in the darkness, he peered out and searched for a form. The slight moonlight allowed Tyler some vision, but nothing could be seen near the garbage. Finally, he made out a small animal on the far side of the bait. He aimed the flashlight and turned it on. The light's beam was reflected in two small eyes near the ground.

"Shit," Tyler said. "A damn skunk."

The animal quickly scurried into the nearby brush, and Tyler directed the light to the pan with the utensil inside. He placed the utensil back in its place and returned to the bedroom. Brenda was sitting up in the bed, with her hand placed over her mouth to stifle laughter.

"Not funny, Brenda," Tyler said, pretending to smack her smiling face. "Lousy damn skunk—can you believe it?"

Brenda, still laughing, reached for Tyler, pulled him to her, and gave him a big hug. "Come here, you big, mean skunk hunter. You are one tough hombre."

Tyler was laughing too, and the two of them lay down, joking for some time before becoming silent and falling asleep.

The alarm remained undisturbed the rest of the night. The skunk had fled the area, never realizing how close it had come to a tragic, brutal death.

Chapter
Twenty-five

After breakfast, Tyler spent a little time exercising his knee. It did not seem to be getting better. He would give it another week or so, and if no improvement was apparent, he would be forced to make another trip to town. If surgery was necessary, it would mean spending a lot of time away from the cabin, the thought of which didn't appeal to Tyler. Brenda suggested that perhaps a trip to the warm pool would help his knee feel better. Tyler agreed.

The couple put their swimming suits on under their Levi's, threw on jackets, and headed down to the bathing pool. The water felt great. Nearly an hour later, Tyler's knee felt better. When they emerged from the warm water, the cool autumn air surrounded their clean bodies, making them shiver.

"Invigorating, huh, Brenda," Tyler said.

"Feels great, Tyler," she responded as she bent over to wrap her wet hair in a towel.

Once the bathers had dressed, they headed back to the cabin, strolling hand in hand, enjoying the beautiful view of the snow-covered mountain peaks in the distance.

"I feel like a ride, Brenda. Want to join me?"

"Sure. Just a short one, though," she said.

The wet swimming suits were hung to dry on the makeshift clothesline Tyler had erected, which consisted of a rope tied tightly between two trees. It wasn't real attractive, but it served its purpose well. Brenda packed a light lunch, and they mounted the ATVs for a leisurely ride to enjoy the beautiful fall scenery.

The ride was wonderful. The trip was slow, as the riders picked their way through the brush and rocks around the lake. Brenda enjoyed riding like this, but Tyler was usually a little more adventuresome. However, with his damaged knee, he enjoyed the slow ride. Brenda led the way, and Tyler followed close behind. While

Brenda scanned the distance for wild animals, Tyler studied the ground. He was checking for signs that the bear had visited again.

Several deer bounded from the brush across the lake into the larger trees, seeking cover. They were beautiful, with full, thick winter coats. Healthy and sassy, the deer stopped periodically to check on the intruders to make certain they weren't getting too close. Little did they know these riders on ATVs were their friends. Brenda and Tyler didn't notice any bucks, but they had read that male deer are more nervous and skittish than does. When wilderness observers spot deer, they are usually does. A buck normally detects the arrival of intruders much quicker than a doe, which senses that the male will alert it if danger arises. The buck sneaks to the cover of large trees or brush, and is seldom detected by the human eye. The doe, on the other hand, is not as careful, but generally stays close to the alert male.

Tyler and Brenda had read that large male deer lose their heavy antlers near the end of winter. The antlers separate near the base, at the point where they are attached to the skull. The buck rubs its antlers against trees to loosen them for the annual shedding. This is referred to as "scraping." Each winter, the antlers are shed, and when spring comes, the males and females look the same. One distinguishable characteristic of the buck is its size. Normally, a mature buck exceeds the size of a doe by as much as twenty to twenty-five percent.

In early spring, the buck begins growing its new antlers. Each year, the antlers get a little thicker and longer. In the early stages of growth, they take on the appearance of being fuzzy; this stage is called "velvet." The buck remains in velvet until late spring or early summer; then, the antlers lose their soft, fuzzy coat, and their texture becomes hard and brittle, ready for battle. In the spring, wilderness observers often find the discarded antlers, usually near an aspen grove, as the soft bark of those trees works well for rubbing and butting to loosen the antlers.

Brenda and Tyler completed their ride, returning to the cabin in the afternoon. Tyler's knee was tiring and starting to throb. He needed to elevate it and rest for a while.

Brenda poured Tyler a shot of bourbon and handed it to him. "Here's your medicine," she said, grinning as she set it on the table.

The ride had made Tyler tired, and he was feeling a little melancholy and sorry for himself. "Thanks," he responded. He looked away, feeling a little guilty for needing the services of a nurse. "I sure wish my knee would start feeling better," he said. "I'm getting a little tired of this limping around and having to depend on you so much to take care of me."

"I'm happy to take care of you, Tyler. But if your knee doesn't get better soon, I think we should make another trip to town and have it checked again," she said.

"We'll give it a few more days, Brenda, and if it's not improved, we'll head to town, okay?"

Tyler finished the bourbon and became very relaxed as the warm tingly feeling spread through his body. The bourbon was not a cure, and Tyler knew it. However, it did dull the pain and give his mind a needed rest.

I can see how people get dependent on this stuff, Tyler thought as he stared into the empty glass. "Can I have another?" he asked.

Brenda took the glass from Tyler's outstretched hand and responded, "Maybe a short one, you lush."

She returned with the bourbon in one hand and a glass of wine in the other. "I'll join you," she said as she sat down on the floor beside his elevated leg. Bud, too, was laying near Tyler, as if to assure him that he was there to help.

"Going to set up the bear alarm tonight, Tyler?"

"Why not?" Tyler said. "If that damn bear shows up around here, I want to know it."

When it got dark outside, Tyler limped over to the fireplace and reached for the moose timber, which he used as a sort of crutch-like cane to assist his movement.

"I'll build a fire and set the bear alarm." Tyler wadded some paper and placed some kindling over it. He struck a match and ignited the loosely structured mass. Soon, the fire was blazing. The warmth it provided felt great. The cabin had cooled while they were out riding, and the heat from the flames felt good on Tyler's body. He placed some larger pieces of wood over the blazing fire.

Just then, Bud jumped up and bolted toward the door. The hair on his back was standing up. Bud placed his nose near the bottom of the door and began to growl.

"What's wrong, Bud?" Tyler asked, working his way over to the window.

Peering outside, Tyler spotted the source of Bud's concern. Standing near the porch of the cabin was a cow moose and a yearling calf.

"Settle down, Bud, everything is fine."

The cow moose had heard Bud growling and turned to trot a few feet down toward the lake before stopping to check on her calf. "Come here, Brenda, take a look," Tyler said. "It's a cow moose and her calf."

By this time, the moose had gathered the calf to her side and was headed down to the lake, with her head held high and her ears standing erect to detect any danger that may threaten her.

"Get your camera, Brenda," Tyler said. "We need to get a picture of these two. They're beautiful."

Brenda left and returned shortly with her camera. The moose had traveled nearly a hundred feet before stopping. Both the cow and the calf were facing the cabin and looking at it.

"Here, Brenda, hand me the camera," Tyler said. He opened the cabin door and crept as quietly as he could out onto the porch, then peeked around the porch enclosure and raised the camera to his eye. He clicked the camera's shutter.

The noise from the automatic film advance frightened the cow. Head down, she charged the cabin porch, sending Tyler into quick retreat. The damaged knee slowed him, but it took only a few seconds for him to get inside the cabin and slam the door. Once there, Tyler hobbled over to Brenda, who was staring out the window. Directly outside stood the huge cow moose, wild-eyed, pawing the ground as if daring them to come out. Tyler and Brenda backed cautiously away from the window and stood completely still, not knowing quite what to expect. The cow moose, having spotted her reflection in the window, swung her huge head and hit the glass with the side of her long head. The window exploded, sending glass flying across the inside of the cabin.

Tyler grabbed the rifle and hobbled back to the broken window with the butt placed firmly against his shoulder, ready to fire. Bud went wild, barking and running around the inside of the cabin in a rage. The barking added confusion to the event, and Brenda started screaming. Tyler approached the window cautiously, his eyes moving quickly from side to side in search of the moose, which had disappeared from view. He hobbled over to the window on the other side of the cabin and caught a glimpse of the cow and calf retreating into the tall brush a short distance from the cabin. Tyler dropped the rifle to his side and turned to Brenda.

"You okay?"

"Yes, I'm fine, just a little confused," she said.

"I can't believe she knocked our window out. I should have shot her!" Tyler said as he hobbled over and placed the rifle back in the corner. The rest of the daylight hours were spent sweeping up glass and nailing boards over the window opening. The bear alarm was set, and the wilderness inhabitants retired for the night.

All remained quiet that evening. Brenda, Bud, and Tyler slept some, though not very soundly. Bud was nervous, and he paced the floor periodically, checking to make sure the danger was gone. Every hour or so he would leave the bedroom, walk into the kitchen, sniff around, and return to collapse at the foot of the bed, exhaling loudly, as if signaling that everything was fine.

The next morning, Tyler's knee was no better. It appeared that it had swollen some during the night.

"We must go to town and have it checked, Tyler," Brenda said as she prepared breakfast.

"Sounds like a good plan," Tyler said as he sipped his coffee. "We need to get glass for the window while we're there."

Brenda knew that Tyler was concerned about his knee and was not excited about making a trip to town.

"We'll take one trailer with us to haul the window back," Tyler said.

After breakfast Tyler measured the opening and jotted the window size on a piece of paper, and they prepared for the journey.

The ride to the Waltons' ranch was uneventful, though it was extremely painful for Tyler. Travel was slow, as Tyler tried to ride the ATV with his leg outstretched as much as possible. Each bump caused him to grimace in pain as the vehicle worked its way slowly down the mountain. Brenda rode close behind, sympathetic to the pain that Tyler must be enduring. The trip took much longer than most of the previous trips. Finally, they arrived at the ranch, and both of the riders felt welcome relief.

The Waltons were surprised to see Tyler and Brenda so soon. After a little time explaining the moose incident, Tyler showed his swollen knee to their friends. Tom and Betty expressed their sympathy, agreeing with Tyler that his decision to see a doctor was a good one. After more light conversation, Tyler and Brenda loaded Bud into the pickup truck and headed to town.

The doctor's office was busy when Tyler and Brenda arrived. The receptionist advised that they had plenty of time for lunch before Tyler would be able to see the doctor. The couple walked to a small diner down the street and ate a light lunch—a cup of navy bean soup and a sandwich for each of them. Tyler barely finished his soup and only nibbled at his sandwich. Brenda knew he was in pain when he pushed the half-eaten sandwich away and gazed into the coffee cup, which he was slowly stirring with a spoon.

"Hurts that bad, huh, Tyler?"

Tyler looked at Brenda and responded, "It's throbbing like crazy. I can't even eat—I'm sick to my stomach. I feel like hell."

Brenda finished her sandwich and Tyler paid the bill. They returned to the doctor's office and waited. At last they were called inside, and Tyler was examined.

"Tyler, I'm sending you over to the hospital to have this x-rayed before I give you my assessment of the damage," the doctor said. "It looks strange to me, and I would like to have an x-ray before I finalize my recommendation."

The doctor picked up the phone and dialed the hospital. "Ted, this is Dr. Howard. I'm sending a gentleman over there with a knee problem. I want a series of x-rays. Full series, if you could." He paused. "Great, I'll send him right over, and he'll wait for the pictures. Send them back with him. Thanks, Ted."

Dr. Howard hung up the phone and turned to Tyler. "Ted over in x-ray is expecting you. Wait for the pictures and bring them back to me." The doctor scribbled instructions on a prescription pad and handed the sheet to Tyler. "See you in a little while."

The x-rays were completed and placed in a large manila envelope. Ted handed the packet to Tyler and asked him to deliver it to Dr. Howard when he got back to the clinic. When Tyler and Brenda arrived, the waiting room was empty. They were ushered into an examination room to wait for the doctor.

A few minutes later, Dr. Howard entered the room and placed the x-rays on a viewing screen.

"Right here, inside the knee—see this little crooked line?" He pointed to an irregular line that commenced at the upper knee joint and traveled about three inches up the inside of the femur. "Here's the problem. You have a break in the lower femur bone. It's actually a crack, but it's serious, nonetheless. It's going to require a cast to heal properly. The crack should heal in four to six weeks, if we're lucky."

Brenda rolled her eyes and looked at Tyler's disappointed face. She said, "It doesn't surprise me. I knew it was more serious than Tyler thought."

The doctor opened the door and called the nurse, to assist him with the application of the cast. He asked Tyler to remove his Levi's and proceeded to prepare his leg. After thoroughly cleaning the area to be covered, the doctor wrapped the knee comfortably tight with a bandage and applied a thick cast, which started six inches below the crotch and extended to about eight inches below the knee.

When the job was completed, the doctor washed up and explained to Tyler, "You'll have very limited activity, and must do a lot of resting. The knee should be elevated above the waist for at least an hour each day. Come back in six weeks and I'll remove the cast."

Tyler attempted to pull his Levi's on, but the cast was too large. "Now what, doctor?" he asked.

The doctor grinned and continued to write on Tyler's medical chart. "I guess you'll be buying some sweat pants, Tyler."

"Now that's real cowboy attire," Brenda said, and winked at Tyler.

With newly acquired sweat pants and a pair of crutches, Tyler, Brenda and Bud drove over to their home in town to spend the night before riding back to the cabin. Tyler hobbled into the house and built a fire while Brenda went to the store to buy some groceries. After dinner, Tyler and Brenda lounged on the couch in front of the fireplace and talked about the broken leg.

"Perhaps we should stay here for a few days, Tyler," Brenda said.

Tyler replied, "I'll be fine, Brenda, and I prefer to be at the cabin."

The next morning, after buying the glass for the window and a few other supplies, they climbed into the truck for the ride back to the Waltons'. With the cooler weather, more perishables could be purchased and kept in the storage area below the cabin. Fresh fruit and vegetables would be a welcome change.

Chapter

Twenty-six

Tom and Betty were waiting when Tyler and Brenda arrived at their ranch for the return trip to the cabin. Tom looked at the cast and said, "Doesn't surprise me, Tyler. I figured you had either a badly torn ligament or a broken leg. You're better off with it broken, believe me. I had a torn ligament once, and I didn't think it would ever heal."

Tom's comments were respected by Tyler, but with the handicap of the crutches and the uncomfortable cast, Tyler couldn't believe that a torn ligament could have been any worse. "This damn cast is a pain in the butt, but I guess I'll have to learn to live with it," he said. "Riding the ATV this way ought to be a real challenge. But I'll have to try. It's about time to hit the road, Brenda. You ready?"

Tyler was right; riding the ATV was an awkward experience. With his leg extended over the riding pegs, there was no way to get comfortable, and travel was very slow—so slow, in fact, that Bud opted to walk alongside them instead of riding in his box. Brenda followed Tyler as usual, pulling the trailer with the window glass and enjoying the scenery as she slowly picked her way up the mountain trail behind her courageous leader.

They arrived back at the cabin and parked the ATVs under the overhang on the side of the shed. Once inside, Tyler hobbled over and built a fire. The cabin had remained secure in their absence, but it was extremely cold. In a few minutes, the fire was roaring. It felt great, but it would take some time to warm the cabin. To speed up the process, Tyler also built a fire in the cookstove. The fire would also be used to prepare the evening meal.

The next project was the installation of the new window glass. Brenda helped quite a bit, running back and forth for tools while Tyler completed the task. The job went smoothly, and they were pleased with the work when they finished.

After dinner, Tyler and Brenda sat in front of the glowing fireplace and read the newspapers and magazines that they had purchased in town. Tyler especially enjoyed reading the newspapers. He hadn't kept up with current events, and was happy to find out that the market was still strong and his investments were doing well. Before retiring for the evening, he pulled the cord to his animal alarm tight and placed the utensil in the pan, just in case the bear decided to make a social call.

Sleeping was not easy for Tyler after the cast was added to his leg. It made comfortable sleeping positions hard to find. The animal alarm remained silent that night, and Tyler awoke the next morning to the aroma of freshly brewed coffee. Brenda had risen early and was curled up in front of the fireplace, enjoying a cup of the steaming liquid, when Tyler pulled on his sweat pants and hobbled into the room.

"Good morning, 'crip,'" Brenda said. "Did you sleep well?"

"Yes, after I finally got comfortable," Tyler responded.

Brenda smiled. "Look outside," she said, pointing to the new front window.

Tyler hobbled over to the window, spread the curtain, and saw that the outdoors was totally covered with snow.

"Looks like it's been snowing for quite some time," Brenda said. "It's probably going to keep it up for a while, too."

Tyler continued to look out the window, as if the falling snow had hypnotized him. Finally, he dropped his hand, allowing the curtain to close. "I'm not sure I'm ready for this," he said. "It's really coming down, and the wind is starting to blow. Better gather some wood and get ready for what looks like a dandy little storm. It may be a blizzard."

Tyler poured a cup of coffee and set it on the table to cool while he dressed for the venture outdoors.

"I'll help," Brenda said. She, too, put on warm clothes, and called for Bud to join them. The couple spent about an hour on the job. Tyler hobbled slowly with the assistance of his crutches, while Brenda did most of the work. After the wood was placed on the porch, the couple took a leisurely stroll down to the lake. The weather was getting cold, and the wind was starting to pick up. Tyler and Brenda were witnessing the start of a good old Wyoming blizzard.

Returning to the cabin, Tyler had to struggle to make it up the hill with his crutches on the fresh, slick snow. At one point he lost his footing and fell to the ground.

Brenda quickly rushed to his side and leaned over him. "You all right, Tyler?"

Tyler reached up, grabbed Brenda by the collar, and pulled her to the ground, laughing and rolling on top of her. Reaching behind his back, he grabbed a big handful of snow and smashed it directly into Brenda's pretty face. Brenda was determined to get even. The two rolled around, laughing and playing like teenagers. The frolicking snow fight lasted for several minutes, and ended when Tyler planted a lustful kiss on Brenda's lips. Eventually, the two made it to their feet; with each other's help, they limped into the cabin. Inside, the playful frolicking turned passionate.

The wind and snow persisted all day, and looked as if it would last all night. Tyler placed several logs on the fire. The stones around the fireplace were now warm, and they would heat the bedroom well, as planned. Tyler got up several times during the night to put more wood on the fire.

Morning arrived, and the storm was still in progress. Nearly a foot of snow had fallen, and the wind had caused huge drifts to form around the cabin. The temperature had dropped into the teens and ice was beginning to form on the lake. Winter was now upon the wilderness inhabitants, and its arrival presented new challenges. It was exciting.

The area was beautiful, covered with the pure white snow. It was an entirely different landscape than what they were accustomed to. The change added a new dimension to the environment, and would provide a drastically different topic for Tyler to capture on canvas. Painting the snow scenes was an exciting experience for Tyler, and he immensely enjoyed the new adventure. The newly fallen snow added such beauty to the scene that even Brenda was trying to paint now. She was not quite as quick to grasp the art as Tyler had been, but she enjoyed it nonetheless.

The snow continued to fall for three days and nights. Tyler's best estimate was that as much as twenty to thirty inches had piled up, and the drifts were four to five feet high around the cabin.

It was time for Tyler to remove the snowmobiles from the shed and put the ATVs away until spring. He started the snowmobiles and drove them outside, then brought the ATVs into the shelter.

The snowmobiles were placed under the overhang of the shed, ready to ride when needed.

Tyler decided that a little test drive for the vehicles would be the event of the day. He found riding the snowmobile a little awkward with the cast, but he was able to get comfortable by sliding his bottom to the rear of the seat, leaving his leg extended forward behind the windbreak. Bundled warmly, Brenda and Tyler mounted the vehicles and took a short, slow ride down to the end of the lake. The vehicles handled the deep snow wonderfully, and Tyler was impressed at the ease with which they maneuvered.

Not bad, Tyler thought, feeling good that they were able to get around so well. The two rode the vehicles in the area around the cabin for a couple of hours, with Bud mounted on the seat in front of Tyler.

Finally, Brenda decided she had seen enough winter for one day, and headed back to the cabin. Tyler and Bud followed. Tyler put the snowmobiles under the overhang and they went inside, where Brenda would make some hot buttered rum to warm their bodies. They rested in front of the glowing fireplace, sipping the warm drinks.

After a short while, Brenda decided that she should feed her little animal friends. Bundled up, she went out to the rock, cleared the snow from it, and sprinkled an abundant amount of nuts and birdseed on top of it. Not long after she returned to the cabin, the grateful little animals began to reap their harvest. The snow had put an end to their ability to easily find food on the ground, and the meals provided by Brenda were much appreciated. She couldn't help but wonder who had fed her little friends before she arrived.

It was nearing bedtime when Tyler hobbled over to the window and peered at the rock.

"Guess I'd better set my alarm again tonight. This would be a perfect evening to catch a bear snooping around out there." Tyler found the cord to his alarm, put the pan on the floor, and placed the utensil inside. "There, that should do it. Got anything I can use for bait?"

Brenda thought for a moment, then walked to the kitchen. "Here are the leftovers from last night's dinner. Will these work?"

Tyler examined the food in the bucket before responding, "This will be fine." He opened the door and hobbled out to place the food under the cord running from the tree to the cabin. Satisfied that his alarm was ready, he entered the cabin and returned to his chair in front of the fireplace.

Before retiring for the evening, Tyler checked the rifle to make certain it was ready and propped it back in the corner near the front door. Yawning, he said to Brenda, "I think I'll give up for the evening. I'm exhausted."

Brenda glanced up from the book she was reading. "Okay. I'll be along in a few minutes."

Tyler hobbled into the bedroom, and before Brenda had finished the page, the subtle sounds of a man at rest filtered into the living room.

Tyler must have been tired, she thought to herself. Then the animal alarm sounded. Startled by the noise, Tyler swung his feet from the bed and placed them on the floor, sitting for a moment before attempting to stand. He pulled on his sweat pants and quietly worked his way toward the front window of the chilly cabin. It was dark, and Tyler was careful not to make any unnecessary noise. The utensil was banging around in the pan quite loudly by the time he reached the window to look out.

The moon was shining, and visibility was excellent. Standing not ten feet from the front window of the cabin was a huge bear. The alarm had worked. The bear was busy digging around in the snow, eating the food that Tyler had placed there.

Tyler removed the rattling utensil from the pan. He then reached for the rifle and slowly opened and closed the bolt, placing a live round in the chamber. Quietly, he opened the door of the cabin and crept onto the porch, where he had full view of the bear. Placing the rifle to his shoulder, he aimed and pulled the trigger. The sound of the explosion was deafening.

Tyler immediately jumped back into the cabin and bolted the door behind him. The bullet had found its mark. Looking out the window, Tyler could see the bear's huge feet thrashing around in the air. The death-growl of the dying beast made his spine tingle from top to bottom.

Brenda came rushing to Tyler's side. Around her neck was the homemade frame of the painting that hung above the bed. Apparently, the blast of the rifle had caused the picture to come crashing down at the same time that Brenda sat up. As a result, Brenda was now wearing the frame around her neck, and the canvas painting was in shreds.

The sight of Brenda wearing the frame, with her wild eyes reflecting fright, was something to behold. Tyler began to laugh. It was unclear whether he was truly amused, or just woefully relieved to have finally shot the bear.

"I got him, Brenda. Come look!"

Brenda removed the frame from her neck and cautiously approached the window. Tyler retrieved the flashlight and shined the light on the motionless heap of black fur.

"Thank God, Tyler, you finally got him! Is he dead?"

"I'm sure of it," Tyler responded. "He hasn't moved for some time now."

Brenda grabbed the picture frame and held it up to the light. "Sorry about your painting, Tyler. It really was one of my favorites."

Tyler began to laugh again. "I wish you could have seen the look on your face when you came out of the bedroom. What a sight, picture frame and all."

Brenda placed the frame on the floor and leaned it against the wall of the cabin, smiling tentatively. "I think I need a glass of wine," she said.

"Me too," Tyler agreed.

After drinking the wine and laughing more about the picture frame incident, Tyler and Brenda returned to bed, neither of them totally comfortable with the thought of the dead bear lying just a few feet from the front door of the cabin. They slept lightly.

The next morning, Tyler climbed from the bed and hobbled to the front window of the cabin. The dead bear was still there, as he had expected. After a cup of coffee, Tyler bundled up in his warm clothing and left to undertake the project of removing the dead animal. He approached the bear with great caution. Once he was satisfied that the bear was indeed dead, he examined it in great detail. There was no evidence that the bear had been wounded before. This must be a different bear, Tyler thought. It doesn't matter; he won't bother us anymore.

Tyler had to get rid of the carcass. He decided the best plan would be to tie a rope to the bear and drag it away with the snowmobile. Brenda was quick to offer the suggestion of dragging the bear a long way away.

The rope was securely tied to the bear's back legs and fastened to the rear of the snowmobile. The animal was frozen stiff, and wasn't difficult to move. It dragged behind the snowmobile like a tree stump on the frozen snow. Tyler headed toward the end of the lake and around to the other side. When he reached the lake's far side, he headed up the hill and went south, in the direction of the area where the lost hunter had been camped. Tyler had dragged the carcass about two miles from the cabin when he decided that it was safe to discard it. Untying the rope, he kicked the bear's body into a deep ravine.

He felt relieved on his way back to the cabin. The rest of the day was spent celebrating the bear kill and talking about the great "one-shot bear-killer." It was a very enjoyable and special day for Tyler and Brenda.

Chapter

Twenty-seven

Winter was in full swing in the mountains. Night found the temperatures dipping down to zero, and sometimes below. The lake had taken on a new look, with a thick layer of ice covering its surface.

Tyler wasn't surprised to find out that the bathing pool hadn't frozen. Steam could be seen rising from the area where the hot spring surfaced and blended with the frigid air above the lake. When it was time to retrieve water for the cabin, Brenda and Tyler went to the small opening in the ice. A bath could also be taken there. The bathing pool was warm enough, as long as they stayed submersed in the warm water. However, when it was time to get out and dress, being quick was important. Tyler had difficulty in the bathing pool, with the cumbersome cast on his leg. He figured out a way to rest his leg on a rock near the edge of the pool so that he could bathe, partially submerged. His baths were quicker than Brenda's.

With the thick layer of ice on the lake, Tyler decided it was time for him to try his luck at ice fishing. It would be fun, and fresh fish would be a welcome addition to the dinner menu.

Tyler took an ax and chopped a hole in the ice. It was about two feet square on the surface and narrowed to about six inches at the bottom of the hole, near the water. The ice was close to twenty inches thick and was safe to walk on and to ride on with the snowmobiles. After chopping the hole in the ice, Tyler fashioned an ice-fishing rig by attaching a length of fishing line and a hook to a willow branch. He placed this rig into a hole he had drilled in a small log near the edge of the chipped ice. Though Tyler was by now quite a fly-fisherman, bait fishing was a new experience for him. The only thing he could find to place on the hook for bait was cheese. He had read somewhere in a magazine that cheese was acceptable bait for trout. He decided to try the cheese, but wanted to figure out a way to catch some minnows, the most popular bait for ice fishing.

Tyler rolled the cheese into a small ball and molded it around the hook before dropping it into the hole. Next, he tied a red bandanna to the end of the willow stick, so any movement could easily be seen from the cabin if a hungry trout decided to partake of the cheese offering.

No trout found the cheese irresistible on the first day. Tyler made several trips to chip the line loose and open the hole so he could check on the bait.

"Not even a nibble," Tyler announced as he hobbled back into the warm cabin. "I need to catch some live minnows."

After considerable thought, he went to the storage shed and returned with a small section of a window screen. He strung monofilament fishing line through the eye of a needle and sewed the screen into a cylinder shape. On each end of the cylinder, he fashioned a cone. Each cone had a small opening at the point that was secured inside the cylinder.

"There, I'll try this," Tyler said as he proudly held the trap up for Brenda's approval. "I'll put some bits of bread inside the cylinder and drop the trap into the bathing pool. When the minnows enter the trap to nibble on the bread, I'll have them."

A look of doubt surfaced on Brenda's face. "That may be more difficult than trying to catch the fish with the cheese," she said, smiling mischievously at Tyler.

"I'm going to tie a string on the trap and pitch it into the pool. Want to come along?"

"I think I'll stay right here in this nice, warm cabin," Brenda said, stretching her arms above her head and extending her legs. She cautioned him to be careful.

Only a few minutes passed before Tyler returned to the cabin. He said, "Now, maybe I'll have some good bait for tomorrow."

The next morning, Tyler grabbed a bucket from the porch and headed down to the pool to check his trap. Arriving at the pool, he grabbed the string and slowly retrieved the trap from the lake. His eyes lit up as the trap came into view. He had caught three minnows. Dipping some cold water from the lake into the bucket, Tyler transferred the minnows from the trap. He placed more pieces of bread inside, then threw the trap back into the lake.

He arrived at the cabin to the smell of freshly brewed coffee. "Check them out, Brenda," he said, proudly holding the bucket so that Brenda could look inside. "I caught three. This should be enough to get me going."

Tyler placed the bucket on the floor next to the door and sat down at the table for a warming drink. Later, he grabbed his min-nows and hobbled out onto the ice to chop the fishing line loose.

Chopping the hole open again was almost as difficult as it had been the first time. The hole had frozen nearly all the way to the bottom during the night. Once the line was loose, Tyler hooked a lively minnow near its tail and dropped it down through the hole into the freezing water. He knew that hooking a minnow in this fashion wouldn't hurt it and would allow it to swim around. The movement would attract the fish—at least, that's what the book he read implied.

Tyler returned to the cabin and was hauling firewood up to the porch when Brenda opened the door and yelled, "You have a bite, Tyler! Look at the willow!"

Tyler turned to see the bandanna on the end of the willow pole bouncing wildly up and down, signaling the first catch of the day. As quickly as he could, he hobbled down to the lake. He grabbed the pole and pulled the fish out on the ice. He had caught a nice two-pound cutthroat.

Tyler returned to the cabin, proudly holding the fish high in the air so Brenda could see it. "Fresh fish tonight," he said. "I'll clean him in a minute, but right now I want to go put another minnow on the hook."

Three big fish were caught that day. Catching more minnows was a slow process, but Tyler had nothing better to do. Ice fishing was fun and productive, and it provided a lot of entertainment and excitement for Tyler.

Tyler and Brenda decided to catch a stash of fish and freeze them for future eating. Obviously, freezing the fish was no problem. Tyler built a freezer box with a secure lid in the storage shed. Brenda added a few other frozen items that had been kept under the firewood on the porch.

When Tyler wasn't fishing, he continued to capture the little minnows. He had caught several, and they were kept in the bucket inside the cabin. They darted around, and Brenda fed them crumbs and cornmeal. The minnows were doing quite well in their new environment.

As much as Tyler enjoyed the challenge of ice fishing, the work required to keep the hole free from ice proved to be quite a task. He was unable to get down on his knees due to the cast on his leg, and cleaning the chipped ice from the hole was difficult. He decided to fashion an ice scoop by putting a large wire hoop on a long stick and sewing more of the window screen across the opening. Though crude and not too pretty, it was quite functional. Tyler was now able to chip the ice loose and remove it from the hole while standing upright.

Another activity Brenda and Tyler enjoyed was riding the snowmobiles on the frozen lake. The ice was perfectly level, and the cushion of snow provided superb footing for the snow machines. Bud loved riding on the snowmobiles. He even started riding on Brenda's machine. He would stand with his hind legs on the seat and his front paws on top of the windshield. He loved riding, and barked profusely as Brenda and Tyler sped across the frozen lake on the fast machines.

The happy little family had learned to love the winter. It brought with it a feeling of comfort and security. Their fear of the bears had begun to subside. Tyler had read that a hibernating bear seldom comes out of its cave until spring is near. However, on rare occasions, bears could be seen rousing in the dead of winter, probably due to hunger. During hibernation, the pulse and metabolism of a bear will slow down until it has almost stopped. The fat stored during the summer will slowly be used up, normally lasting until spring. When a bear finally comes out of hibernation, it will be very hungry and have an unhealthy appearance. It will feast on anything available. Since food may be scarce, the bear will often be required to travel long distances to find food. This is when bears would be seen coming down from the high mountains and into the meadows. Ranchers would have to keep a keen eye out for bears during lambing season, as a bear can really wreak havoc on a herd of newborn lambs.

Now it was winter, and the bears were in retreat. Tyler, Brenda, and Bud put thoughts of the bears behind them.

Chapter
Twenty-eight

The snow and angry weather continued, and a feeling of despair began to overtake Brenda and Tyler. It seemed like the snow would never stop. Many days were spent just hanging around the cabin, frantically searching for something new and different to do. Tyler painted, and Brenda tried her hand at various crafts—anything to make the days as short as humanly possible. It was hard to make every day a new adventure.

Magazines were read and reread from cover to cover. Picture puzzles were put together, taken apart, and put together again. Cabin fever was overcoming them, and even smiling became difficult. The long winter nights were almost more than the couple could tolerate.

Brenda was keeping a diary. It seemed to her as though she was going to perish in this environment, and she wanted the people who discovered her frozen body to feel the pain and discomfort that she had felt in her last few days of life. Living in this cold winter hell was intolerable, and she thought there was no way she could survive the ordeal.

Brenda had given up painting, as Tyler's God-given talent gave her a feeling of deficiency and defeat. Tyler's work continued to amaze her. It seemed as though his hands were guided to put the proper touch and adornment to every scene that he attempted to capture. It came so naturally and easily to him. Every stroke of the brush seemed like it was meant to be. Brenda was a bit jealous, but was truly impressed with his talent.

Brenda and Tyler obviously loved each other. The winter couldn't have been a better test of their love. What was it that made Tyler seem so perfect and right to Brenda? When coping seemed impossible, Tyler would come through and give Brenda a feeling of comfort and security that only true and undying love could provide.

Could it be having Tyler all to herself in a comfortable world of serenity that gave her such a sense of security, or was it simply that they were really meant for one another? Brenda didn't care. She was just glad they were together.

When the weather permitted, Tyler, Brenda, and Bud spent time outdoors, making the most of the environment they had chosen. It helped them to stay sane and healthy during the long, cold winter.

Tyler was sitting in a chair and soaking up the heat from the fireplace one day when he decided that it was time to remove the cast. His leg was feeling better. Though the doctor had given him explicit instructions to return to his office for the cast removal, Tyler was convinced that he could do it himself. He told Brenda that it made no sense for them to go to town when he could take care of it at home.

Tyler left the cabin and returned with a small saw and a pair of tin snips. He sawed and snipped the cast, starting from the top and slowly cutting his way to the bottom, then separated the stiff plaster and cautiously removed it from his leg.

"There, it's off. I knew I could do it," Tyler said. He began to rub and scratch the itchy leg; this felt great. He had been burdened with the troublesome cast for six weeks, and without it Tyler felt like he had been born again. He was ready to face the world and tackle anything that came along. He stood cautiously and placed weight on his leg to test it.

"It feels great, Brenda. Want to do some 'shit-kicking'?" Walking with a slight limp, Tyler paraded around the cabin. The leg was a little weak, but there was no pain.

For the next few days, Tyler exercised his leg, attempting to build the strength that the leg had lost. The leg responded well, and its original strength and dexterity slowly returned. It had healed, and Tyler was soon walking and maneuvering as well as ever.

"Welcome back, good leg," Tyler said one night as he rubbed his recovered knee. "I think this calls for some celebration. How about a little bourbon, Brenda?"

Ice fishing was one of Tyler's favorite things to do now that he was unhindered—free of the bulky, troublesome cast. Brenda and Tyler ate fish prepared in just about every way—broiled, fried, and even smoked. Tyler had created a smoker by placing a small cabinet constructed of wood over a bed of smoldering charcoal. Though crude, the smoker proved to produce edible—even delicious—fillets of fish. The smoked fish kept well, and could be carried easily when they explored the outdoors. Riding on the snowmobiles was a great pastime, and enabled Brenda and Tyler to see parts of the beautiful mountains that they could never have seen without them. Many days were spent exploring trails, to see where they led. Most turned out to be game trails, which ran from one water source to another and wove through meadows where the animals grazed and rested. Brenda and Tyler got to know their way around in their little private world, and had become comfortable leaving the cabin to explore, having no fear of becoming lost.

The long, cold winter was relentless. There were days when the highest temperature was still below zero. The nights were long and extremely cold, creating a huge demand on the wood supply. It was starting to appear as though Tyler had not stockpiled enough wood to make it through the winter. They were down to their last cord, and spring was still over a month away. Tyler decided he must cut more wood.

The next couple of days were spent cutting and splitting the precious fuel for the fire. Wood cutting was a much bigger chore in the deep, cold snow. Tyler became acutely aware that they must have wood to survive. The fear of running out was all the drive that Tyler needed to find the strength to work in the inclement conditions.

With the fish Tyler was able to catch and the large cache of stored food from town, their food supply was quite ample. However, the stock of bourbon was less plentiful, much to Tyler's dismay.

The days continued to drag on. Long, overcast, gray, gloomy hours were still the standard. As much as Tyler and Brenda loved each other, they found themselves becoming a little testy with one another. Tyler tried desperately to inspire happy times for the two of them, but would often find himself staring into space, worrying about what the next day would bring. Brenda had read every magazine in the cabin at least three times. Each moment of the day seemed to last an eternity. Would winter ever end? Even the mountains and the beautiful, serene setting were turning into a gray, dismal picture. Bud also sensed the tension. The three of them could only sleep so much. It seemed like things were about to explode. Brenda was starting to wonder how much she really loved this little paradise that they had found. Could she make it through another month?

After two more weeks of winter agony, it appeared that the weather was about to change. The sun was starting to warm up the landscape during the daytime, and the deep snow was beginning to melt. The change was a welcome shot of enthusiasm for the three mountain dwellers. Brenda and Tyler found themselves smiling again. It looked like they would successfully survive the winter and make it to spring. A feeling of true accomplishment kindled in Brenda and Tyler. They had handled the long, tough Wyoming winter, and now felt they could survive forever in the wilderness.

The days became brighter, and a sense of "soon-to-be-spring" blossomed in the mountains. Only Brenda, Tyler, and Bud could fully appreciate their feelings of exuberance and accomplishment. Tyler often found himself covered with goose bumps when he thought of their success in wintering the wilderness. He was truly happy, and most of all, he was proud of Brenda. She had stuck this thing out, fully demonstrating her support and undying love for him.

A new feeling of life warmed the hearts and lives of the wilderness inhabitants. The days continued to get longer, and the temperature was above freezing during the day. Even the squirrels and chipmunks were back, searching the rock for food. Brenda was quick to spot them, and provided her little friends with an abundant feast. It wasn't long before every critter in the area was pecking around the rock. Brenda had made several friends.

The warmer weather brought other wild animals out, searching for food. One evening, near dusk, Brenda spotted a new visitor to the rock.

"Tyler, come here and look," Brenda said. "What is that little guy?"

Tyler approached the window and searched the area, then spotted the creature. "That's a 'possum," he said. "He's become a new member of our hungry little clan." Tyler tapped his finger on the window, and the little visitor was gone as quick as a flash.

Tyler referred Brenda to one of the wildlife books on the shelf. She read that the 'possum, or "opossum," its proper name, is one of nature's most interesting creations. It is North America's only marsupial, or pouched animal. Breeding of its young takes place in an amazing way. The female opossum has two wombs, and to accommodate this, the male sex organ is forked. The opossum's gestation period lasts for a mere twelve to fifteen days. The babies, called "porcupettes," are born without eyes; their ears are barely developed, and there are only the smallest resemblance of rear legs. The entire litter could be placed in an area the size of a quarter. A normal litter includes around a dozen porcupettes. The front feet of the newborns have tiny toenails. These are used to climb through the mother's fur and find the way to the pouch on her stomach, which has several tiny teats. The newborns attach themselves to a teat by swallowing it. Once the tiny animals are attached to a teat, the pouch provides a very secure world. For two months, the little animals remain in the security of the pouch, attached to a teat.

Finally, when the babies are about the size of a mouse, they begin to explore the inside of the pouch and find their way out. However, at the first sign of danger, they scamper back inside, to safety. More and more, the babies venture out of the pouch, riding on the back of their mother. The mother will lay her tail over her back, and each of the youngsters wraps its tail around hers to hang on while she travels around. Eventually, the young will leave the mother's back and scratch around in the dirt for food. Three to four months after birth, the youngsters finally wander off on their own.

A mature female, Brenda learned, weighs five to seven pounds. A mature male is larger—usually between ten and twelve pounds. The female opossum has as many as three litters a year, but only a few of the offspring will likely reach maturity.

Brenda read on. The animal had probably derived its name from the common expression "playing possum," which meant to feign death or unconsciousness. When confronted, an opossum will lay inert on its side, with its eyes closed and its mouth open. In this condition, one can pick the animal up by the tail and carry it around as if it is dead. It was once thought that this was a defense mechanism of the opossum, but it was later learned that the animal is actually experiencing a form of paralysis. If left alone, the animal will eventually regain consciousness and waddle away. The opossum is also special in that it is the only animal in North America with a prehensile, or grasping, tail. Its tail can wrap around a tree limb and actually support the weight of the entire body. The opossum also has a diverse diet, eating nearly anything to insure its survival.

Chapter
Twenty-nine

Early one afternoon, while Tyler and Brenda were out for an afternoon walk, Bud again came across his most seriously hated enemy—the unconquerable, dastardly, deadly porcupine. Tyler caught the flash of the charging dog out of the corner of his eye just in time to spot the target of Bud's attack. Bud leapt on the porcupine, his mouth open, growling furiously. The porcupine rolled over once. Bud was immediately on top of it, grabbing the animal with his teeth and attempting to tear its flesh. However, the penetration of the quills was just too much for old Bud. He released the animal and rolled over on his side, laying motionless and in severe pain. The porcupine scrambled to its feet and quickly exited the scene. Brenda and Tyler ran over to their friend. Bud was in trouble. The penetrating quills, probably thirty in all, completely covered his mouth and head. One of them had punctured Bud's right eye, and several more had penetrated his breast and rib cage. It was a sickening sight. Tyler gently placed his hand on Bud's side. Bud was conscious enough to recognize Tyler's touch and kicked wildly in the air, trying to get up on his feet. Then, pain forced Bud into a motionless state of trauma.

Brenda placed her hands over her mouth to hush the mournful sound that was trying to escape her body. She was shaken, and it was apparent that Bud wouldn't be with them much longer. Tyler examined their little friend's limp body before shaking his head and looking solemnly into space, fighting the tears that were building in his eyes. He ran his fingers tenderly up and down the dying animal's back. Tremors of unwelcome death overtook Bud's body. The dog drew three deep breaths, then totally relaxed, closed his eyes, and placed his head against the soft earth for the last time. Bud was gone.

It had all happened so fast. It seemed unfair. Tyler raised his body up on trembling legs and stood there, slowly shaking his head in disbelief. Brenda wrapped her arms around his neck and stood in silence as the tears poured from her eyes. Tyler let his tears go and joined her. The two of them stood in each other's arms in total disbelief and sorrow. Their friend Bud was gone. His life had been ousted from his body so quickly and so painfully. One of the quills had found its way into Bud's chest cavity, undoubtedly puncturing the heart of their faithful friend. Tom Walton was right—though it seemed to be a small and docile animal, the porcupine had taken the life of their best friend.

"Damn, stupid, ignorant porcupine," Tyler said. "I can't believe it. I simply can't believe it."

Several minutes passed before Tyler pulled away from Brenda and looked into her swollen, tear-filled eyes. "Brenda, I'll carry Bud to the cabin. We'll bury him. If only I could have seen the porcupine in time, I could have kept Bud away. It's probably my fault."

"It's not your fault, Tyler. It had to happen sooner or later. Bud hated them so much."

Tyler reached down and picked up the limp, motionless body, then slowly headed back to the cabin. Once there, he searched the surrounding area and picked a spot under a small pine tree, then lay the animal's limp body on the ground.

Brenda watched as Tyler dug a hole and placed the body of their good friend inside. After a pause, Tyler filled the hole and piled the remaining loose soil in a small mound on top of the grave. He leaned on the shovel and stared at the mound. Brenda stood by his side, resting her head on Tyler's shoulder.

"I'll really miss him, Brenda," Tyler said.

"Me too, Tyler. I loved him."

Brenda reached for Tyler's hand and slowly led him to the cabin's porch. Tyler paused briefly to lean the shovel against the front of the cabin before entering, then walked into the kitchen to pour himself a shot of bourbon. The couple commiserated in silence.

The next day, there was continued mourning over the loss of their companion. Before the day was over, Tyler had fashioned a marker and placed it at the head of the beloved animal's grave. He had skillfully carved Bud's name onto it before placing it in the ground. Tyler stood there for some time, reminiscing about how he had found Bud, and reliving various events in their time together—

how Bud would ride in the box mounted on the rear of his ATV, how Bud would follow him up and down the creek bank while he fished, and the many times that Bud could be seen peering out the window of the cabin to welcome him when he returned. Bud had become a part of life for both Brenda and Tyler. His memory was entrenched in their minds, and he would be sorely missed.

Tyler looked away, and a slight grin passed over his lips. "Enjoy yourself in heaven, old buddy. Hope God enjoys you as much as we have."

The next morning, Brenda and Tyler were finishing their coffee when Tyler noticed the little animals eating on the rock scattering for cover. He got up from his chair and walked over to the window.

"It's Tom and Betty!" Tyler pulled open the front door and greeted their guests. "Hello, folks! What brings you up to this part of the world?"

Tom, climbing down from his horse, smiled at Tyler and said, "Thought Betty and I had better come up and see if you two had survived the winter." Tom shook Tyler's hand, then gave Brenda a kiss on the cheek. He pushed her back at arm's length and quickly scanned her from top to bottom. "God, it's great to see you both. Looks like you wintered well. Brenda, you look no worse for wear. Maybe a little thinner, but it looks like you came through okay."

Tyler helped Betty dismount from her horse. He led the two horses over to a limb hanging from a nearby tree and tied them securely. "Come on in. We'll make a fresh pot of coffee and bring you up to date on the happenings up here in the wilderness."

Brenda spent a short while in the kitchen before returning to the dining table with four steaming mugs. The two couples sat around sipping coffee and discussing the winter's events for quite some time. Tom and Betty were sad to hear about the loss of Bud.

"Damn porcupines. I tried to warn you that Bud wouldn't learn his lesson and leave those critters alone," Tom said. "Seen it happen many times before. Porcupines have been responsible for the loss of many good dogs, including a couple of mine. And while we're discussing unfortunate events, I should warn you that a bear, or perhaps two, have taken down nine of my newborn lambs in the north meadow. Haven't seen the bastards, but I'd say there are at least two. Stay alert—they could show up around here most anytime."

Brenda looked over at Tyler, then dropped her head, staring at the floor. She despised the thought of having to contend with the bears again. If anything would drive her from this wonderful country, it would be them.

The visit with Betty and Tom was enjoyable and provided Brenda and Tyler with a renewed outlook on life. Their friends couldn't have arrived at a better time. The loss of Bud had made them sad, and the fresh, cheery visit from the Waltons was badly needed. Brenda felt a little empty as Tom and Betty mounted their horses for the ride back to the ranch. "Come back soon," she said as she waved good-bye.

Tyler and Brenda stood with their arms around each other, watching the Waltons ride away and disappear into the trees. They turned and slowly walked hand-in-hand back to the cabin. They had grown to care for the Waltons, and their visits were always welcome. That evening was spent planning the details of a trip to town. The thought of the trip made Brenda feel good. She needed to be around other people. It had been a long, lonesome winter, and a break in town would be great—not to mention a good dinner with all the trimmings at a local restaurant.

Brenda and Tyler spent the next day preparing for the trip. Much of the snow was gone, and Tyler decided the snowmobiles wouldn't be practical for the trip, so he removed the ATVs from the shed and filled their tanks with gasoline. One trailer would be taken to bring back the supplies. The shopping list had gotten quite lengthy, as they had used up most of their necessities during the brutal winter.

Tyler was also visibly happy to be going to town—in fact, in his joy he had overdone it on the bourbon. Brenda couldn't help but laugh as she watched him from the kitchen window—moving the little trailer around to align it and hook it to the back of his ATV. As he maneuvered, his foot slipped in the mud, and down he went. Tyler landed right on his butt in the slimy, wet mud, and sat there for a few seconds before laying back and beginning to laugh.

Brenda opened the cabin door and tried to be serious. Half laughing, she asked Tyler, "Did you hurt yourself, you idiot?"

Tyler rolled over on his side and raised his body up on one elbow. Turning to Brenda, he asked, "Would you come help me up?"

Brenda stepped through the open door and extended her hand to Tyler, who slowly reached up and grabbed her hand, then gave it a firm yank and pulled her down on top of him. He rolled Brenda over, pushing her face into the mud. Soon they were mud wrestling, and there was no winner. When the ordeal was over, both Brenda and Tyler were covered with mud from head to toe. A trip to the bathing pool was the only way to clean up the awful, sticky mess. Brenda tiptoed into the cabin and got towels, shampoo, and soap. They headed for the lake.

Tyler was forced to use Brenda as a stabilizing aid as they walked. The bourbon had made moving with any sense of direction impossible. He laughed and tried to talk along the way, but his words made no sense. If Brenda didn't love him as much as she did, it would have been very easy to shove him into the bushes and leave him there. Instead, she did her best to keep him upright.

The water in the bathing pool was warm and felt great. Brenda shampooed her hair and scrubbed off the mud while Tyler lounged in the pool and blew bubbles in the water. He was a mess. After Brenda completed her bath she began to shampoo Tyler's hair and wash the mud from his body. The task was finally completed; amazingly, Tyler hadn't drowned. Brenda dried her body and wrapped a towel around herself, then pulled her drunk friend from the pool and dried him off before helping him put his sweat pants on. The trip back to the cabin was not much easier than the trip to the lake had been. Brenda had about ten pounds of wet clothes to carry, as well as having to provide a leaning post for her companion. Back at the cabin, Brenda guided Tyler to the bedroom and helped him get in bed. Tyler was motionless for the rest of the evening.

He was not too chipper the next morning. Brenda had risen early, and drank several cups of coffee before she went into the bedroom to see if Tyler was still alive.

Tyler grunted a few times and rolled over, looking at Brenda through half-opened eyes. "Damn, what happened? Tree fall on me?"

Brenda reached down with one hand and ran her fingers through his tangled hair before responding. "I think it may have had something to do with that empty bourbon bottle sitting in the kitchen. I think you were over-served. Want to get up and get ready to go to town?"

Tyler lay there staring at the ceiling, his eyes squinting and straining. "What time is it?"

Brenda moved her right hand from behind her back, where it had been hidden, and suddenly smashed a huge handful of snow directly into Tyler's face, then rubbed it vigorously. "It's nearly nine o'clock, you lush!"

Tyler was now awake, and very much alive. "Brenda, that was a bold move—you will pay for that with interest, you beast!"

Laughing wildly, Brenda quickly retreated to the kitchen to await Tyler's arrival, while he scrambled around the bedroom trying to get dressed—a difficult undertaking, considering the way his head was throbbing. Standing up was a monumental challenge.

Mostly dressed, with great effort, Tyler made it from the bedroom to the kitchen table. Here, he would rest and try to get a cup of coffee down before attempting any more serious movement. Once he was certain that his heart would continue to beat, Tyler pulled on his boots and stood up.

"I'm ready to go to town, you demon," he said.

Brenda smiled as she pulled on her coat for the trip. This feat would most likely be much easier for her than for Tyler.

The trip was tough for Tyler. It seemed as though the wheels of the ATV were made of stone. Every little bump in the trail jarred his head and made his vision blur. Brenda, knowing Tyler was suffering, had just enough of an ornery streak in her to ride fast, forcing him to keep up. Many stops were made along the way so Tyler could take a trip down to the stream and dowse his face with ice-cold water.

"Brenda, if you see me trying to drink any more bourbon, I want you to take that moose timber and hit me right between the eyes. Will you, please?" he begged.

Brenda nodded her head and smiled mischievously before saying, "Sure, old buddy, be glad to."

Finally, the Waltons' ranch came into view. The ride had seemed several hundred miles long to Tyler, and he was ready to get off the ATV, which normally was great fun to ride. Tom and Betty were not around, so Tyler and Brenda got into the truck and headed into town. Brenda drove.

Chapter

Thirty

Brenda and Tyler accomplished several things on their trip to town. First, Tyler called Chicago to see how his investments were doing, and the report was favorable. Then, he decided that perhaps he should see the doctor and let him know that he had removed his own cast.

While Tyler was taking care of his doctor's visit, Brenda had a few projects of her own to accomplish. She had brought five of the paintings that Tyler had completed, and wanted to see if they would sell. Her aim was to share the beauty that Tyler was able to put on the canvas with the rest of the world. All she had to do was find a gallery that would accept the paintings on consignment. This turned out to be a simple task. The first proprietor she spoke to liked Tyler's work, and was obviously quite impressed. This made Brenda feel proud.

The shop owner, a woman named Tracy, invited Brenda to the back room of her shop for a cup of tea. After Tracy had jotted down a few notes, she thanked Brenda for bringing in the art and vowed she would do her best to sell it. Brenda had to trust Tracy to be honest with her, since she had no way of knowing what price the art should bring. The tourist season was not far away, and the timing was perfect for the consignment of Tyler's pieces. Brenda advised the shop owner that she would check in the next time she was in town and see things were progressing.

Next, Brenda purchased some personal items and some clothing. She used to love buying clothes, but hadn't shopped for them in over a year. She had more interest in practical items now. She filled two large shopping bags with clothing, and enjoyed every minute of her shopping trip. She also purchased a few items of badly needed clothing for Tyler.

Brenda and Tyler spent the better part of a week in town before deciding to head back to the cabin. Tyler had fully recovered from the "bourbon flu" and was feeling much better.

The Waltons were sitting on the porch when Tyler and Brenda arrived. Before loading up the trailer, the couple visited with Tom and Betty. Then, they decided they needed to get on their way.

Tyler enjoyed the ride back up to the cabin much more than he had the trip down. He and Brenda stopped several times, admiring the beauty of the countryside. The wildlife was abundant; along the way they spotted a deer with her fawn, a moose with her newborn calf, a coyote, two foxes, and nine head of elk.

It just doesn't get any better than this, Tyler thought as he picked his way up the muddy trail on his ATV. Brenda was riding in front, and Tyler followed, pulling the trailer loaded with the supplies.

The couple arrived back at the cabin and found everything in good order, just as they had left it. Their little animal friends were scampering around the rock, waiting to be fed. Brenda couldn't make them wait any longer, so she dug into one of the shopping bags and brought out a huge bag of sunflower seeds for the animals. Quick as a wink, the rock was covered with their furry little friends.

While Brenda fed and watched the little animals, Tyler explored the perimeter of the cabin for signs of the bear. He tried to be as discrete as possible. He knew that if he showed any sign of concern, Brenda would be worried, and he wanted her to enjoy the homecoming.

Tyler didn't see anything out of the ordinary around the cabin, but it did appear as if something had scratched on the rear door. The scratches were near the bottom of the door, indicating that it had been a small animal. Probably a porcupine, Tyler thought hopefully.

Tyler armed the bear alarm again that evening. The alarm was quiet all night, perhaps because they had no garbage to put out for bait. Many animals in the wilderness can smell garbage for quite some distance and will venture close to check. Most can be scared away with light or sound, with one exception—the bear.

The next day, Tyler was sitting at the table when he noticed several deer, elk, and a couple of moose trotting down from the mountains and across the lake, as if they were being herded. They seemed to be in a hurry. Tyler walked over to the window to see what was going on. He pulled the curtains back and looked toward the head of the lake. He was startled to see that the lake was covered with smoke.

Tyler pulled the door of the cabin open and ran outside. The pungent smell of smoke filled his nostrils. The smoke seemed to be coming from a fire that had started just over the small mountain at the head of the lake, and appeared to be working its way toward the cabin.

Tyler knew that he and Brenda had work to do. "Brenda, come see this!" he shouted.

Reaching the door of the cabin, Brenda saw the fire and began to panic. They had to prepare the cabin and their belongings for a forest fire. Now, that's a good one, Tyler thought. How do you prepare a cabin for a forest fire?

They must assume that the fire would come around to their side of the lake and could burn the cabin and storage shed. They needed to get as many of their personal belongings as they could out of its path. Tyler went inside, sat at the table, and began jotting a plan on a sheet of paper. First, they would ride the snowmobiles from the storage shed down to the beach and out into the water, about twelve to eighteen inches deep, where the vehicles would be safe. Next, the tools and supplies must be wrapped in tarps and buried in the sand near the lake. Brenda was to bring the items from the cabin that she wanted to save, which would also be buried. They could use the ATVs to evacuate the area. The cabin and storage shed were at the mercy of God, if the fire came their way.

It was nearly noon by the time the tools and personal items were securely buried in the sand and the snowmobiles had been safely placed in the lake. Tyler quickly reviewed the items left in the cabin before closing and locking the door. He then nailed pieces of roofing tin over the windows. The smoke was getting more intense, and an occasional flame could be seen rising through the dense clouds. The trees near the head of the lake were encompassed by flames, and it looked as though the fire would come around the lake on both sides.

Tyler and Brenda had done all they could to protect and save their worldly belongings. They now had to ride the ATVs to safety and let fate take its course.

"God save our little cabin," Brenda said as she rode away from the smoke and down the trail to the Rocking R Ranch.

When they arrived, they found Tom and Betty anxiously awaiting them.

"I knew you would come, but I didn't know exactly when," Tom said as he walked out on the porch to welcome them. "I've been in touch with the forestry department, and they told me that the fire was started by some hunters over on Black Butte—spring bear hunters. Fire's already burned a thousand acres, and if the wind doesn't change it'll get more. The upper fire line has finally reached the snow, so that side seems to be in check. Did the fire reach the cabin?"

"Not quite, Tom, but it's not far away," Tyler said. "I could see flames up by the head of the lake when we rode out."

"We'll stay in touch with the forestry department—they're flying over the area regularly, plotting the course of the fire," Tom said. "We'll ride up there in the morning on the ATVs to see what's going on. Right now, we might as well relax and have a drink. There's absolutely nothing we can do."

The two couples watched the glowing red horizon; they could smell the smoke from the front porch of the ranch. They sat with a portable radio, watching the fire and tracking its progress. The news wasn't favorable.

Eventually, the tired observers decided it was time to retire for the evening. Neither Tyler nor Brenda slept well. They kept thinking about the time and love they had invested in the construction of their cabin, and the possibility of losing it and their beautiful trees and little animal friends.

When daylight filtered through the parted curtains in the room where they were sleeping, Tyler was the first out of bed. He dressed and walked into the living room, where he found Betty and Tom having a cup of coffee.

"We may have gotten lucky, Tyler," Tom said. "I think the winds shifted to the north around midnight last night, and my best guess is that the fire may have gone around the other side of the lake."

"God, I hope so," Tyler said. He poured himself a cup of coffee and went out onto the porch to have a look. The smoke from the fire was hanging in the air down in the valley and leading up to Eagle Lake. Tyler could see it billowing up in the distance as the fire worked its way to the south, along the upper rim of the mountain. "It's hard to tell from here, Tom. Maybe we should take a ride up that way and see if we can determine whether Brenda and I still have a home."

After breakfast, Tom, Tyler, and the two women sat on the porch and watched the steady stream of smoke bombers attacking the fire. Tom explained that the old military aircraft had been converted to carry the red-colored slurry used to fight forest fires. They were upgraded with turbo engines, which gave them more power for high altitude performance. He added that the pilots of these aircraft are a cross between a half-drunk sailor and a neurotic brain surgeon. They fly their aircraft just above the treetops, dumping the fire-retarding slurry directly on the fire. Tom told Tyler and Brenda that they could be seen flying right into a box canyon to dump their slurry, then pulling the nose of the aircraft up to roll back over and return in the direction from which they had come. "These guys have balls," he said.

The slurry bombers continued to fly for most of the day. The BLM had set up refilling facilities at the local airport, and the planes weren't gone long before they returned with another load of the red slurry.

Finally, Tom and Tyler could stand it no longer. They had to check on the cabin—or on the area where the cabin had once stood.

The sight of Eagle Lake was a welcome relief. Apparently, Tom had called it right. It appeared that the fire had turned, forced by the north wind to the other side of the lake. The cabin side of the lake had fewer trees, so the fire had stayed up higher, on the back of the mountain. There was little damage around the cabin. Tyler was relieved.

Tom and Tyler dug up the tarp containing the tools. Each of them grabbed a shovel and set out to check for small, smoldering spots that could ignite and start the fire blazing again. They spent the better part of the remaining daylight hours searching for those spots and shoveling dirt on them to keep air away from the smoldering wood.

Happy and tired, Tyler and Tom rode back to the Waltons' ranch to share the good news. Brenda and Betty were jubilant to find out that there had been no damage to the cabin, or to the trees in the immediate area.

The fire was still burning on the side of the mountain across the lake from the cabin. Tyler and Tom listened to the radio. It was reported that over four thousand acres of timber had been consumed by the fire, and that two hundred full-time firefighters had been unsuccessful in extinguishing it. The best relief they could hope for would be a good old-fashioned rainstorm. The brisk northern wind had saved the cabin, but was driving the fire south much faster than the firefighters could contain it.

Brenda and Tyler decided to spend one more night with the Waltons before riding up to Eagle Lake and their home.

Chapter
Thirty-one

Coming home to the cabin the next day was a joyous event. The couple got to work right away. They retrieved the snowmobiles from the lake and put them in the storage shed. All of their belongings and tools had been dug up and put away in their proper places. The cabin had acquired an obnoxious smoky smell, both inside and out. Brenda opened every window and both doors to air it out. The smell diminished each day, and the sky eventually cleared. The fire-fighters had finally been successful in arresting the fire.

After a few days of cleaning the clothing and belongings inside the cabin, things returned to normal for Brenda and Tyler. With the ice now gone from the lake, Tyler was ready to catch some fresh fish for dinner. As usual, catching fish wasn't a problem for Tyler—in fact, he caught six nice trout and released them before deciding to keep two large cutthroats for dinner.

After breakfast one morning, Brenda and Tyler decided it was time to ride over the mountain across the lake and explore the burned area. When they got there, Brenda was appalled by the devastation the fire had wreaked. There were no trees left standing, only occasional large stumps where the fire hadn't burned a tree down to the ground. Smoke was still rising from a few of the large piles of burned timber. The small fires would smolder for several more days, or until a mountain shower wet them down. Tyler and Brenda rode in awe for several miles, surveying the damage.

As they picked their way out of a canyon along a steep trail, Brenda got careless and let the left front wheel of her ATV climb up on a boulder about eighteen inches in diameter. The trail was steep, and the added height of the boulder was more than the vehicle could handle. The front of the ATV came up, and the vehicle rolled over. Brenda screamed as she fell, but Tyler had already crested the hill and didn't hear her.

Tyler continued to ride across the meadow for some distance before realizing that Brenda had not made it out of the canyon. He quickly turned his vehicle around and headed back. From the brim of the canyon he was able to see the ATV lying on its side, about one quarter of the way down. Tyler scrambled down to Brenda, who was lying face down several feet above her ATV. She was unconscious. Apparently, she had hit her head on a boulder during the fall.

Tyler turned Brenda over onto her back and examined her eyes. Her pupils were dilating—a good sign. He patted her on the cheek and called her name.

Brenda finally opened her eyes and stared at Tyler. "What happened?" she asked.

"That old ATV tried to eat you, Brenda. Lie still for a while. Do you have any broken bones?"

"I don't think so, but my head is throbbing," she answered, rubbing the left side of her temple. "Wow! Put your hand here."

Tyler placed his hand on the left side of Brenda's head. "You have quite a goose egg. Now, lie down and get your breath while I see if I can get your ATV up here."

Tyler quickly uprighted the vehicle and got it started. It had lost little gasoline, and although there was some cosmetic damage to the vehicle, it appeared that it could be ridden back to the cabin.

Tyler quickly maneuvered the ATV up the remainder of the hill and shut it off. He then went back for Brenda, who was feeling a little better. Tyler slowly helped her up. "Let's see if you can stand," he said.

Brenda walked apprehensively at first, but it soon became apparent that she had no serious injuries, and she was able to walk to the ATV. Tyler would keep an eye on her for the rest of the evening.

They rode slowly on the way back to the cabin. One mishap a day was enough.

They spent the evening relaxing around the cabin. Tyler talked excessively to Brenda to prevent her from going to sleep, since he was concerned about the bump on her head. By eleven o'clock, both of them were ready for bed. Tyler set his alarm clock to wake him at one o'clock. He reset it to wake him at three o'clock and again at five o'clock so he could check on Brenda. If he couldn't wake her during any of his checks, it would probably mean she had a concussion, and he would have to figure out a way to get her to the hospital. Fortunately, she was easily awakened during all three checks and seemed fine, except that her head was sore and badly bruised.

The next morning, Brenda found movement a little tough. She was stiff from her tumble. Tyler was not accustomed to waiting on Brenda and taking care of the other chores by himself. Brenda was a good patient, however, and wasn't too demanding of Tyler.

It was only a day or so before Brenda had received all the nursing she could handle. She had to get out and get some fresh air. The couple decided to take a short hike up to the edge of the lake and assess the damage the fire had inflicted on the timber down the back of the mountain. The sight of the damage was sickening. The fire had wiped out every standing tree all the way down the side of the mountain and across the meadow below. Brenda and Tyler just stood there and stared.

Finally, Tyler broke the silence. "Incredible, huh, Brenda. Can you believe it?"

"I can't believe it, Tyler. Our beautiful trees are gone." Brenda looked away as tears filled her eyes. She was a lover of life, and the loss of the trees was just as serious a loss to her as the loss of the life of an animal or any other living thing. She had seen all she wanted to, and without another word she turned to leave.

On the trip back to the cabin they didn't speak. Brenda was sad, and Tyler knew the best thing he could do was let it rest.

The couple was startled when a doe and her newborn fawn bolted out of the trees and worked their way down to the edge of the lake in the direction of the cabin. This took Brenda's mind off the fire and put the sparkle back in her eyes. She was happy to see new life, and took comfort in the thought that her little friends were still around and would return to the rock for food.

Back in the cabin, Tyler busied himself with capturing the mother deer and her beautiful little fawn on canvas. Only a person with no heart or sense of love for life could ignore the helpless innocence of a newborn fawn, he thought. Tyler worked well past dark, frustrated with his lack of success in making the picture as descriptive and detailed as he wanted. He had hoped it would grab the viewer as much as the original sight had grabbed him just a few hours earlier. Realizing that the light from the lantern was inadequate, Tyler abandoned his efforts for the evening. He would have to continue another time.

Feeling frustrated and tired, Tyler decided to arm the bear alarm and call it a day. He was still a little apprehensive about the possibility of a bear returning to the cabin. Once the alarm was set, Tyler gave Brenda a peck on the cheek and retired to the bedroom.

He fell asleep and drifted into dreamland, but was awakened by an abrupt, noisy movement in the other room. He found Brenda wildly swinging the broom around near the ceiling, her eyes frantically searching.

"A damn bat got in here, and it's flying all over the place," she said in disgust.

Using his flashlight, Tyler found the intruder hanging from a ceiling timber. The little bat was hanging upside down, contentedly minding its own business. Tyler slowly moved a chair below the hanging critter and hit it with the broom. The bat hit the floor, and Tyler swatted it a few times before reaching to pick it up. The little creature was stunned. Tyler walked over to the door and tossed the uninvited guest onto the roof outside the cabin. The bat would likely gather its senses, crawl over to the edge of the roof, drop, and fly away.

Tyler explained to Brenda that bats are interesting little creatures—they are like mice with wings. They have terribly sensitive eyes, and light bothers them. Because of this, the bat does most of its hunting for food during the night and normally sleeps during the day, keeping its eyes closed to protect them from the light. The bat's diet consists mostly of flying insects, and insects as small as mosquitoes will often suffice to satisfy its hunger. Though somewhat of a pest, the bat is helpful in controlling the insect population. A bat can eat up to several hundred insects a night. Bats are conveniently equipped with elaborate sonar systems that enable them to zero in on flying insects and catch them with lightning speed.

Tyler continued by explaining that the one shortcoming of the bat is its inability to launch into flight. The bat is thus compelled to land high enough on a limb or a perch to allow it to drop, catch itself with its outspread wings, and fly away. If a bat ever lands on a flat surface, it must climb up on something so it can fall before it can fly.

Bats also tend to live in colonies, Tyler explained. Once they have found a home, they will continue to use the same shelter for years. If a bat gets into a house, that is where it will live and raise its young. The homeowner will one day discover that his or her house is infested with a colony of bats—several hundred is not an

uncommon number. Once a house is infested with the little creatures, the only way to get rid of them is to find their entrance and
plug it late in the evening while the bats are out eating. However,
the entrance holes are often very difficult to find, since a bat can
squeeze its entire body through a space as small as a dime.

Though harmless to humans, bats can often be the carrier of
diseases such as rabies, Tyler added. The threat of disease is actually
the biggest concern. Though not aggressive, the bat does have teeth,
and can bite if it is about to be harmed.

The next morning, Tyler found the entrance hole the bat had
used and plugged it before the critter returned with a couple of
friends and decided to start a family in their cabin. Brenda had
made it clear that she had no desire to share her home with a family of creepy little bats. Of all the new friends she had made since
her arrival in the wilderness, the bear, the bat, and the porcupine
were the only ones she wanted to keep away from her home.

Chapter

Thirty-two

Tyler and Brenda had spent nearly a whole year away from other people and were very close to each other. There had been few personality conflicts and personal differences between them. The uncomfortable times they had encountered had generally been fueled by some uncontrollable happening of fate or inspired by forces outside of their relationship. Tyler felt sincere, devoted love for Brenda, and though he had not made a legal commitment to her, he felt a magnetic attraction to her. Her welfare and happiness were a constant concern to him. Brenda, on the other hand, had a strong desire for a formal commitment from Tyler. It wasn't that she didn't trust him, but her upbringing and morals dictated that she should be officially married. Also, she felt a certain sense of insecurity. What assurance did she have that she had any claim to the man she loved? What would prevent him from leaving her anytime he wanted to? Their different needs did not create insurmountable problems for Brenda, and Tyler didn't even know they existed.

Brenda spent a lot of time studying their relationship. Where was it going? How would it end, if it did? Would she live in this cabin in the wilderness forever with Tyler? Would they ever move back to the hustle and bustle of the big city? Would she ever be blessed with a child? Would the fantasy wear off and create feelings of emptiness? These things were important to Brenda, and she dedicated many hours of thought to searching her mind for answers. However, she never questioned Tyler about their future. She didn't want to make him feel uncomfortable. Things were great between them, and Brenda didn't want her concerns to raise questions in Tyler's mind.

Spring finally arrived, and the beautiful mountain wildflowers bloomed in beautiful shades of red, yellow, blue, and pink. Brenda and Tyler spent many hours strolling around the huge mountain meadows, planting the gorgeous scenes deep in their memories. These were the moments that made the whole exercise of their independence worthwhile.

On one of these nature walks, the couple stumbled upon a fawn that had apparently stepped into a hole and broken its front leg. The leg bone hung pitifully below the knee, attached only by the skin on the outside of the leg. Feeling sorry for the little animal and wanting to help, Tyler and Brenda planned to capture it. Tyler would sneak through the willows and position himself beside the trail leading away from Brenda, who would then approach the little fawn and try to force it to retreat down the trail. Once the fawn was within Tyler's grasp, he would jump from the willows and capture the little animal.

Their plan worked to perfection. After Tyler wrestled the fawn to the ground, he and Brenda tied its legs together and carried it back to the cabin. At first the little fawn was scared, and wildly tried to flee. After some unsuccessful attempts to break away, the animal's injured leg forced it to settle on the ground in total submission.

Tyler examined the broken leg and decided how he would cast it. After some thought, he came up with a plan. First, he would fashion a splint out of green willow branches. Next, he would surround the broken bone with several of the small branches and wrap them with cotton string to hold them in place. He would wrap several layers of gauze over the cotton string for strength and support. With any luck, this would hold the bone in place while it mended.

The fawn seemed nervous and apprehensive about accepting his new acquaintances, and most of all, it was unsure about the makeshift splint on its leg. Tyler tied the fawn's three good legs together to keep it off its feet while it became familiar with the newly applied splint. The little fawn soon became tired and defeated, and quit thrashing around on the cabin floor and attempting to get back on its feet.

Brenda and Tyler tried to get the fawn to eat. They encouraged it to try a few bits of lettuce and some fresh carrots. Being held and fed by alien hands was a frightening experience for the small fawn, but it was hungry and eventually ate the vegetables. Later, the fawn lay on its side, closed its eyes, and fell asleep. It slept for nearly three hours before Brenda and Tyler heard it thrashing, trying once again to stand. The fawn had no success, and eventually settled down.

The next morning, Brenda and Tyler found the little animal lying almost content, as if it had given up any hope of escape and was willing to accept whatever happened. Again, they fed the little animal and caressed it. The fawn appeared to be feeling a little more comfortable with the human influence in its life. Tyler examined the splint placed on its leg and decided to see if the animal could stand. Unfortunately, the fawn was still apprehensive about its environment and tried again to escape the confinement. Tyler was afraid that the animal would hurt itself even worse if it was allowed to walk. He decided to put the constraints on its legs for a while longer.

On the third day, Tyler was able to get the fawn up on its legs and help it stand. The little fawn cautiously placed its weight on the splinted leg and began to move slowly around the inside of the cabin. Before the day was over, the animal had adapted to the splint and was moving gingerly around on the grassy area outside the cabin.

For several days the fawn remained outdoors, tied with a rope. At night the fawn was moved inside. It ate the food placed before it and could move around quite well. Tyler and Brenda decided it was time for the fawn to sleep outside.

The fawn had become quite comfortable around the humans, and was no longer afraid. Brenda and Tyler's new friend was a robust companion. Wherever they went, the little fawn would hobble along. It had developed a strong sense of security among them, and behaved as though it were a full-fledged member of the family.

For several weeks, the fawn was allowed to hobble around with the splint firmly in place on its leg. The day came when Tyler decided the leg was probably healed. It was time to remove the splint. Tyler removed the outer wrapping, the string, and the green willow splints from the fawn's leg, then released the fawn to see if it would walk. Though a little shaky and wobbly, the small deer began to move briskly around the area. Only a slight limp could be detected in its stride. The splint had worked. Tyler was proud. He had managed to save the fawn, which probably would have been dead in a few days if Tyler had not intervened.

The fawn became an adopted member of the family. In the evening it would stand outside the cabin and peer in the windows, appearing to want to come inside. In the morning, the fawn would eat whatever Tyler and Brenda offered it.

Life went on as usual around the cabin. Tyler continued to paint during the day and fished nearly every evening. The deer had become quite a buddy to Tyler, and followed him around like a puppy. The young fawn had picked a small grassy area near the storage shed where it would bed down at night. It was almost as if it was there to take the place of Bud. Though Tyler and Brenda never mentioned Bud to each other, he was in their thoughts nearly every day.

The fawn matured, and gradually took on the appearance of a mature male deer. The time that the little buck spent around the cabin was diminishing. One day, it became apparent that the deer had adapted to the wild and no longer needed the security that Brenda and Tyler provided. The whole ordeal had been a satisfying experience for the couple—knowing that they were able to contribute something to the survival of one of the animals they had learned to respect and adore.

The question that continued to haunt Tyler was, had they done the animal a favor? The deer had become used to being around humans and wasn't afraid. How long would this little buck last, once hunting season began? The thought worried Tyler, but all he could do was hope that the animal would survive.

One afternoon, as Tyler was scanning the area behind the cabin with binoculars, he spotted a wilderness inhabitant that is seldom seem—the sharp-shinned hawk, commonly called "the sharp-shin." This hawk is quite common in the state of Wyoming, but is seldom seen by man. Tyler learned that sharp-shins are the smallest of the North American hawks. The bird has partially rounded wings and a long, straight tail. The combination of short wings and a long tail benefits these birds by allowing them to fly through very small openings in dense growth. It is joined in this by the similar-looking Cooper's hawk and the much larger northern goshawk. These three are the only hawks found in the area of Wyoming where the couple lived.

Though abundant, sharp-shins are rarely seen in the summer. In early spring they begin a reclusive life in thick pine forests at higher elevations. The sharp-shin gets its name from a raised ridge on the front of the bone just above its foot. About twelve inches in length, it is a small bird of prey. It commonly hunts birds smaller than a dove. It is this desire for small birds that offers humans a chance to view the hawk. The sharp-shin, contrary to most birds of prey, does not fly high and attack its prey from above; rather, it can be seen flying lazily behind a group of small birds, as if it is not interested in them. However, if one of the birds attempts to land or appears fatigued, the sharp-shin swoops up as quick as a flash and grasps the bird in its talons.

The life of a sharp-shin is mostly spent under dense cover, darting around in search of small birds. That is why seeing one is difficult. Tyler had recognized the bird from his reading, and though he saw it only briefly, it was a delightful experience. Many times, a sharp-shin can be seen in urban areas. The hawk has learned that the common practice of feeding small birds such as finches, waxwings, and sparrows has made residential bird-feeders a smorgasbord. Spotting the sharp-shin was a new experience for Tyler. He was pleased to have identified another of his native friends.

Chapter

Thirty-three

Brenda was sipping a cup of coffee when Tyler crawled out of bed and joined her at the table. Leaning over, he kissed her on the cheek and asked, "What are you doing up so early this beautiful morning?"

She replied, "I don't know. I just woke up early and couldn't go back to sleep, so I made some coffee and decided to read for a while."

Tyler poured himself a cup of coffee. "What shall we do today?" he asked.

Brenda shrugged her shoulders and responded, "I don't care, but it's such a pretty day, we should go somewhere."

Gazing out the window, Tyler nodded his head. "Sounds great to me. Where would you like to go?"

Brenda thought for a few moments. "Oh, maybe for a ride. We could head up the ridge and ride the trail south."

"Sounds good to me. Let's do it," Tyler replied.

They finished their coffee, and Brenda packed a couple of sandwiches for the outing. On the ATVs, the two explorers rode around the lower end of the lake, heading up to the ridge that took them south. The ride was beautiful. The wildflowers were in full bloom, and the colors were magnificent. Brenda loved exploring. No rush, no hurry—just relaxed, peaceful riding.

It was about noon when they reached the end of the trail, on a high bluff. The vantage point overlooked a small, beautiful lake surrounded by aspens and huge granite boulders. Brenda dismounted and motioned to Tyler, who had turned his ATV around and was heading back. He had stopped to see what was keeping her. "Come on, Tyler," Brenda called. "Lunch time. Let's have a little picnic."

Tyler reached into the small box mounted on the rear of his ATV and grabbed the blanket that he carried for such occasions.

The two spread the blanket and sat down among the vibrant, sun-warmed grass. They relaxed while eating the sandwiches that Brenda had packed.

Brenda lay back on the blanket and stared up into the beautiful, blue sky. She gazed at the white, puffy clouds and made pictures in her mind.

"Look, Tyler, there's a large sailboat. See it? The big cloud over to the left of the little V-shaped mass."

Tyler lay back and stared up as well. "There, over there, Brenda, see Mount Rushmore? You can even make out the faces."

Brenda and Tyler spent over an hour pointing and laughing at the different shapes and figures their imaginations formed from the clouds. No place in the world had bluer skies than their paradise.

After a while, Brenda turned to face Tyler and lay motionless, staring into his face.

"Tyler, can I ask you something?"

"Sure, Brenda, anything you want. Anything."

Brenda paused, looked away briefly, then turned again to face him. "Do you love me, Tyler?"

Tyler leaned over and kissed her softly on the lips. "Sure I do, Brenda. How could you question that?"

"Oh, I guess I just need to be reminded once in a while."

Tyler moved his body very close to Brenda, who was still lying on her back. He looked down into her eyes. "I never want to be without you, Brenda," Tyler said, reaching up and drawing little circles on her face with his finger.

Brenda smiled at Tyler, then looked away as if embarrassed. She finally sputtered, "How much do you love me, Tyler?"

"Bigger than all the clouds in the sky," he said. "Bigger, even, than the blue in the sky. Is that big enough?"

"Not enough," Brenda replied. "I . . . I want . . ."

"What is it you want to say, Brenda?"

"Well, I think you should know . . ."

"What?"

"Nothing, Tyler. Nothing." Looking around, Brenda spotted a small trail. Pointing to it, she said, "Let's go see where that trail leads. Shall we?"

Brenda jumped up and started her ATV. Tyler gathered the blanket in his arms, stuffed it into the box, and started his machine.

"Follow me. I'll lead the way," he said.

It was nearly four o'clock when the two tired riders arrived back at the cabin. The ride had been wonderful, and Brenda was extremely tired. She fell asleep sitting in one of the large chairs in front of the fireplace. Tyler wrapped a light blanket around her and stretched out on the floor. He, too, quickly fell asleep. He had a pleasant nap, which ended only when the sun had sunk below the horizon. Rubbing his eyes, Tyler was surprised to find the cabin totally dark and cold. Brenda was still sleeping in the chair.

Once Tyler began moving around, Brenda also awoke. She said, "I can't believe we slept that long. What time is it?"

Tyler glanced at his watch and said, "It's 10:15. Time to go to bed."

After a light snack and a glass of wine, the two weary explorers retired to the bedroom to finish their rest. But Brenda was now wide awake, and she couldn't fall asleep. She lay there and stared into the darkness above the bed. Why can't I tell Tyler? she thought. I must tell him. I must.

The next day was warm and humid, and the sky appeared to promise rain. Brenda was not feeling well, and informed Tyler that she wanted to stay close to the cabin. Tyler was a little concerned. Perhaps they had overdone the riding episode the previous day. He stayed by the cabin, looking after Brenda. After all, she was his best friend. Tyler loved her, and he was happy to offer her affection and care.

Chapter Thirty-four

It was a beautiful evening and Tyler was down at the lake, fly-fishing. He was proud to bring three large trout back to the cabin to show Brenda, expounding on his expertise as an accomplished fly-fisherman. After he took a photo of the fish, Tyler poured himself a little bourbon to celebrate. Later, he cleaned the fish and placed them on a stringer, which he hung in a tree to chill. The evenings were still cool enough to keep the fish from spoiling.

Ready to retire for the evening, Tyler set the bear alarm and went to bed. Brenda was reading and stayed awake a little longer. Finally, her eyes got heavy, and she joined Tyler in bed.

It was around two o'clock when they were awakened by the utensil rattling around in the pan. Tyler quickly left the bed and crept toward the front of the cabin. It was a moonlit night, and Tyler was able to make out the silhouette of their unwelcome visitor. Standing on its hind legs and feasting on the three trout hanging from the tree was the animal he and Brenda feared the most—a bear.

Tyler peered out the window for some time, wondering what he should do. Should he try to shoot the animal, or merely frighten it away? Killing the bear seemed rather ruthless. He had already made up his mind that there was no way he could kill everything that posed a threat to their serenity. As he watched, the bear finished devouring the three trout and lowered its body to the ground.

Brenda had arrived at Tyler's side and was staring out the window at the huge, ugly beast. She cried, "Tyler, what can we do to keep them away from us?"

The sound of Brenda's voice startled the bear, and it was gone in a flash.

"I guess the only way is to kill them, Brenda. I'd hate to do that, but if that's what it takes, I'll do it."

Tyler and Brenda stood motionless in the darkness, staring outside at the moonlit wilderness. Finally, Tyler took Brenda by the hand and led her back into the bedroom, where they held each other tightly until they fell asleep.

Neither of them slept well. No matter how hard he tried, Tyler was unable to cultivate a feeling of comfort in Brenda. She was tense and uneasy. Something was bothering her. She acted as though she had something to tell him, but couldn't.

The next morning was dreary and overcast. It was the kind of morning when thoughts of bright city lights and activity seemed exciting. Brenda sipped her coffee and stared out the front window of the cabin. Her thoughts were several thousand miles away. In fact, for some reason she was thinking of a sunny beach scene from several years ago, during college. In her thoughts she was surrounded by several of her best friends, and was sipping a lime-flavored rum drink. Laughter and a carefree attitude filled the air. It was mesmerizing. Brenda was smiling and staring through glazed eyes when Tyler walked up to the table and interrupted her.

Wrapping his arms around her waist, he said, "What's got your pretty face smiling so beautifully?"

Startled, Brenda turned around and looked at Tyler. She said, "You surprised me. I was dreaming about being on a sunny beach down in the Caribbean. Sounds great, huh?"

Tyler poured himself a cup of coffee and sat down at the table. Reaching to pat Brenda on the head, he said, "Wyoming is where it's happening, Brenda. No sandy, tourist-filled beaches around here. If there were, I would be on the next train to Dodge. Are you getting tired of this quiet, peaceful world we live in?"

Brenda grabbed Tyler's hand and placed it against her cheek. "No, Tyler, I love this place, and I love you. However, I must be honest. Without you I would be gone. Tyler, you make this place what it is. There's just something about you and this place that go together. Without you, this place, as beautiful as it is, would be only a memory to me."

Tyler understood what Brenda was saying to him. He knew she was only there because she wanted to be with him.

They read books and stayed near the cabin for most of the day. After a few mountain showers the sun peeked through the clouds, lighting up the lazy countryside. It was almost as if someone had hit a switch that changed the lighting.

Shortly after five o'clock, Tyler told Brenda that he was going to go fishing. Grabbing his fly rod, he headed down to the lake. He studied the water briefly, then turned to head up toward the inlet to try his luck there. Tyler hadn't fished that portion of the lake since last summer. He worked his way through the willows and waded out into the lake nearly up to his waist. With several skillful casts he gently placed the nymph, which was tied on the end of the tapered leader, on the surface of the quiet lake.

No takers, Tyler thought. Perfect presentation of the nymph, and no damn takers.

Tyler continued to work the edge of the lake, hoping an inquisitive trout would sample his meticulously presented nymph. Finally, the tip of the fly rod dipped dramatically, and the adrenaline flowed through Tyler's body. This is a lunker, Tyler thought. Patiently, he fought the large trout. It was both exciting and challenging for Tyler to land this fish. He couldn't wait to show it to Brenda. After a while, the fish succumbed to the talent and relentless efforts of its captor.

Six pounds if it weighs an ounce, Tyler thought as he examined the beautiful cutthroat in his landing net. The bright red streaks coming from the bottom of the mouth followed the deep ruts back to the gills. Beautiful specimen, he thought. Simply beautiful. And indeed it was. All fly-fisherman dream of a catch like this.

Tyler fashioned a fish stringer by whittling the foliage off a long, green willow branch. Then, he ran the willow through the gill of the fish and shoved it through the mouth. Since Tyler had left a rather large stub near the base of the willow branch, the fish was securely affixed to it and was unable to escape. Tyler shoved the branch down into the sand on the shore. The fish was now staked and secure, ready for the trip back to the cabin and the frying pan.

Tyler returned to the lake to see if he could hook another beautiful native. Working diligently and doing his best to make a presentation that would be irresistible to the trusting foe, Tyler lost track of time and failed to notice the diminishing daylight. It became difficult for him to see what he was doing. Suddenly, he realized that it was getting dark. Brenda would be worried, he thought to himself.

Tyler worked his way to the edge of the lake and grabbed the willow stake with his prized catch of the evening. Working his way through the willows, he suddenly felt a cold, overwhelming dread.

The goose bumps were in full blossom from the back of his neck to his ankles. He discovered at once what was causing his discomfort. Standing up on its hind legs, facing Tyler, was his worst nightmare. The bear was huge, standing nearly two feet taller than Tyler, and it had a look on its face that needed no explanation. The bear meant business, and the fish Tyler was carrying added fuel to the fire.

There was no escaping the inevitable, but there were so many things left undone. There were still things Tyler wanted to say and do before he met his demise. He loved Brenda more than anything in the world, and he wanted to be with her forever, to marry her and have children with her. Why hadn't he told her that? Unfortunately, when God beckons, there is seldom time to make up for lost opportunities.

Moments seemed like hours as Tyler stood facing the brutal, insensitive bear. Tyler stood frozen in his tracks. The confident animal slowly rolled its head and let out a bloodcurdling, deafening roar, letting the entire world know that it was the doubtless challenger and ultimate victor of this untimely confrontation. The animal's movements were confidently slow and precise, as if giving notice that it was going to undo the life that stood before it. The bear opened its large mouth, showing its hideously ugly and filthy teeth. The huge, aggressive animal charged the defenseless human standing rigidly before it, swinging its huge claws and growling wildly as it attacked.

Tyler was no contest for the massive beast. The battle was short and violent, and the result was death. Tyler's body was thrown into a bloody, defeated heap.

The huge bear slowly lowered its body to all fours and pushed its nose up into the clammy night air, sniffing for fight and terror. The animal wanted more. It lowered its head and sniffed at its kill. Convinced that its foe was void of life, the bear turned, grabbed the fish, and slowly walked back into the brush, then disappeared into a dense stand of trees.

Chapter
Thirty-five

Finding Tyler's body was the worst experiences of Brenda's life. She discovered the torn, mangled corpse with the aid of the dim beam of the only flashlight she could find. It was a terribly cold, ruthless experience. The only person in Brenda's life whom she had truly loved and cherished more than life itself had been taken from her by a dynamic swat of an animal's paw.

Although she was in shock and scared into a frenzy, Brenda did well in handling the grim situation. She made it back to the cabin and down to the Waltons' ranch before daylight.

Could this really be happening to me? Brenda wondered. Yesterday, she had been with the man she loved in the beautiful country that she had learned to love. Now, they were both memories left in her busy, confused mind.

Several weeks passed after Tyler abruptly exited Brenda's life before she could find enough strength to go back and visit the cabin. She knew it would be extremely hard for her to return, and the journey required every ounce of courage she could gather.

Tom and Betty accompanied Brenda back to the cabin to recover a few things and return Tyler's cremated remains to the country land he loved. There were few things at the cabin that Brenda wanted, other than the moose timber and a couple of the paintings that Tyler had lovingly completed for her. Tyler loved this place, and she felt that he would want her to leave it undisturbed.

After carefully burying the ashes in a shallow grave near the lake, Brenda sat for the better part of the day in a chair, gazing out the cabin's front window. Tom and Betty left Brenda alone as her teary eyes stared into the distance. Her mind was filled with beautiful memories as she relived the time that she had spent with Tyler. Finally, content and satisfied that she had fulfilled her obligation to return to the cabin and pay her tributes, Brenda, with thousands of fond memories sealed in her mind, turned to Betty and Tom and said, "I guess I'm ready."

The trio walked out onto the front porch of the cabin, with Brenda clutching the moose timber tightly under her right arm and holding the two paintings that she loved just as tightly under the other. They slowly walked down to the edge of the beautiful lake. The tragic event had been terrible, and the healing process would be slow.

Brenda was starting to accept the fact that Tyler was gone forever. She made it to a large granite boulder and shakily sat down. Eyes closed, she leaned back against a pine tree and cried. "I can't leave . . . I just can't do it," she said through her tears.

After considerable begging and pleading, Tom and Betty were able to convince Brenda to leave. She must trust that the memories would remain in her mind, they told her. She could never change what had happened. Life up there would never be the same for her without Tyler.

The three of them slowly worked their way back down the mountain. When they arrived at the Waltons' ranch, darkness had fallen, and the cold, damp evening made the sickness in Brenda's stomach almost unbearable. She retired early and quickly fell asleep, only to awaken a short while later. She spent the rest of the night lying motionless, staring into the darkness.

When morning finally arrived, Brenda had found a new enthusiasm for living, for some reason. When she had entered the relationship with Tyler, she had been noticeably insecure. During her time with him, a feeling of security and strength slowly developed within her. She had lived a very meaningful and fulfilling life with him, a life that had created a purpose for living, loving, and caring. Brenda must now go on with her life and live it the way Tyler would have wanted her to—the way he had unknowingly taught her.

Brenda returned to the little rented home in town. Her days were spent sorting through Tyler's things, and each item she handled brought back memories that tugged at her heart. The days were long and lonesome. She spent many hours holding an item such as a shirt next to her heart, gazing into the emptiness of the room, with tears moving gently down her face. She knew that she needed to get rid of her terrible visions of Tyler's death, so she could focus on her fond memories of him and get on with her life.

Chapter
Thirty-six

Nearly three long weeks had passed since Brenda had moved back into the little house before she went downtown to meet Betty and Tom for lunch. The lunch was pleasant, and Brenda felt confident and comfortable as she visited with her friends for a few hours.

After Tom and Betty left to return to the ranch, Brenda decided to look around the small town and see about finding a job to keep her mind occupied. Brenda visited a few art galleries and gift shops, but the owners were busy, and she couldn't find it within herself to interrupt and inquire about work. Feeling lonesome and a little sorry for herself, she decided to give up and return to the rented house. She had driven almost all the way home when she noticed a small, barely legible sign printed on a piece of cardboard—it said, "Free puppies." A spark of enthusiasm filled Brenda's eyes as she quickly and recklessly steered the pickup truck into the small driveway. This was exactly what Brenda needed—a loyal, loving, and compassionate little friend.

The choice was almost automatic. A little brown male with black markings came right up to her. A little Bud, Brenda thought as she picked up the tail-wagging, licking little creature. Brenda's heart swelled. It was as if God had given her a new life.

Brenda's days became filled with happy, playful times. Little Bud was wonderful. Brenda loved her newfound friend, and spoiled him beyond all reasonable limits.

She spent many hours thinking about the little piece of heaven up at Eagle Lake. Her mind would often drift and become lost in thoughts of the grand times she had enjoyed while living there with Tyler. She described her memories to the puppy as if he was capable of understanding everything she said.

She cautioned, "You must always remember, Little Bud, to never ever go near a porcupine. They will hurt you and take your life away.

Never do that." Little Bud would roll his head to the side and look at Brenda with big, sad eyes, just as if he understood every word.

Brenda was getting a grip on her life again, and her confidence had finally returned. She convinced herself that with Little Bud she could survive and be happy for the rest of her life back up on the mountain. The challenge was just too great to ignore.

Brenda told Betty and Tom that she was pregnant. God bless Tyler, who never knew, they all murmured. Brenda knew that she had to return to the mountain cabin, her little piece of heaven. She knew instinctively that she must raise her child near its father. That is where they belonged.